SECRETS on the Lake

Delia Dibble

A catalogue record for this book is available from the National Library of Australia

Publisher:
ASPG (Australian Self Publishing Group)
P.O. Box 159, Calwell, ACT Australia 2905
Email: publishaspg@gmail.com
http://www.inspiringpublishers.com

National Library of Australia Cataloguing-in-Publication entry

Author: Dibble, Delia

Title: **Secrets on the Lake**/*Delia Dibble*

ISBN: 978-1-925908-98-5 (pbk)

Acknowledgement

I gratefully dedicate this book to my loving husband, Jeff, my best friend and soul mate.

He is the first reader (and critic) of my manuscript.

I thank him for his full support, dedication, love, encouragement and the strength he gives me.

And also to my children

Sandra, Carla and Nick

You taught me how to be a mum.

The meaning of unconditional love.

No one will ever love you more than me.

Chapter 1

Today, Laura Menzies is an incredibly successful international Human Rights lawyer for the United Nations. She's an intelligent, intellectual, sensuously desirable woman, who also happens to be very chic. However, very few know of her tragic upbringing at the hands of her alcoholic, drug-addicted parents.

The family lived in a subsidized house in a poor neighborhood in Louisiana; the money paid to the family by the government was used mostly to feed her parents' addictions. Laura and her younger sister, Libby, were very much left alone to care for themselves. They were constantly hungry and forced to search for food in the neighborhood's rubbish bins.

Roger and Emma, the girl's parents, were constantly under the influence of alcohol and drugs; they had sadly become completely ensnared by their addictions. They were never vicious, nor did they physically mistreat Laura and Libby—they were just careless, showed no parenting skills, and were too focused on their own self-destruction. Without any guidance, the girls, aged ten and eight years old, were simply left to the streets to fend for themselves.

The owner of the local bakery shop was a woman named Mary—a jolly woman with large cheekbones who was never to be seen without an apron about her waist and a colorful scarf tied around her head—would give them leftovers that hadn't sold by closing time. "Here! Some cake and extra bread for tomorrow! We are closed tomorrow, girls!"

That was the best—sometimes *only*—meal of the day, which kept Laura and Libby going. But on the public holidays when the bakery didn't open, the girls battled with starvation as they were not able to hide the leftovers. The bread and cake they brought home was taken away by their parents.

"*Everything* is closed tomorrow," Libby said. "Let's try to get more food while we can."

"Where do you want to go?" Laura asked. "I'm tired and it's getting late—we can search the bins tomorrow. Let's go home."

"No!" replied Libby. She looked across at a grocery shop on the other side of the footpath. "Wait here," she told her sister.

Knowing Libby well, Laura was worried about what her sister might have in mind. "Don't do anything stupid, Libby! Let's go home!" she urged.

But, of course, Libby wasn't listening.

The sisters were very different from one another. Laura was quiet, sensible, and cautious while, in contrast, Libby was an inquisitive, devilish, chatty, and an adorable tomboy who just wasn't afraid of anything!

"No, Libby, no! Come back here!" Laura called after her sister.

But Libby had already crossed the road and was walking with intent in the direction of the grocery shop. Wearing her worn-out, washed-out overalls with a striped t-shirt underneath, and old, tattered shoes, the carefree little Libby entered the busy grocery shop. At first, she walked behind a random lady in an attempt to give the impression the lady was her mother. Taking an apple from the fruit bench, Libby hid it inside her pocket. She was grabbing a second apple to hide alongside the other when the owner—a fat, short Greek man with a little mustache and strong accent—spotted her. "Hey! You there, little girl! Come here!" he cried.

The owner had kept a suspicious eye on Libby from the moment he'd spotted her. He doubted very much she was the woman's daughter, as she didn't seem anything like the well-dressed, upper-class lady at all. He was right, of course, and he'd caught Libby in the act!

Libby saw the fat man darting in her direction with his angry eyes blazing. She ducked under the fruit tables and rolled as fast as she could to prevent him from catching her. The owner ran breathlessly around the shop, bending down under the fruit benches trying to spot Libby. But the poor old man was no match for the agile little girl; she was like a wily little hamster, popping her head with its mop of messy, curly hair over the bench as she looked for a way out of the shop.

"You little devil!" the shop owner bellowed out his frustration when he spotted her. "I'll catch you!"

Libby upped and ran so fast she bumped into the other customers. She almost lost her balance as she knocked hard against the fruit racks and tables to send apples, oranges, peaches, and pomegranates rolling across the floor!

She managed to evade the man who desperately tried to grab her as she scampered out of the shop. She even managed to grab some of the scattered fruit from the floor on her way out as the customers looked on. Happy with the little girl's victory, some of them even gave a discreet smile. The owner finally gave up the chase and was left red-faced and puffing. He gesticulated with clenched fists high in the air. "I'll catch you, you devilish little girl!" he yelled after Libby.

From a safe distance on the other side of the footpath, hiding behind a large tree, a shaking Laura chewed nervously on her fingernails as she watched the drama unfold. When she saw Libby come racing out of the grocery shop, she followed her sister—running as fast as she could after her down the street.

When she felt safe enough, Libby stopped. Her heart was pounding hard in her skinny chest as she fought to catch her breath.

Laura caught up with her, desperately trying to catch her own breath. Laura sat down beside her sister and said, "You crazy, crazy girl! One of these days you're going to be caught!"

With an impish smile, her little nose upturned and wrinkling her cute face, the headstrong and vivacious Libby ignored Laura's disapproval. She took out the two apples she'd hidden in her pockets, plus two extra peaches she'd snuck into her bib. "Here," she said with a smile, "we have our dinner!"

Meanwhile, looking at the mess Libby had left behind in his shop, the owner despaired. "Arrr! That poor little girl! She could have just asked—I'd have given her some fruit quite gladly!"

This was the way the two girls lived through most of their days.

Often, they would skip school to search through the rubbish bins so they could eat. Other times, they'd rely upon people's generosity and little Libby's thieving adventures. The latter distressed poor Laura so much, but she couldn't do anything to stop Libby because she was an opportunistic thief who took a risk whenever she saw a chance! However, it was always food she stole—just food and nothing else.

The school principal reported them so often for skipping school, they were eventually removed from their home by the intervention of the Social Security Department and given into the care of their grandmother, Lucy Menzies.

Lucy had a heart of gold and was a very agreeable, sweet woman of sixty-five. Sadly, though, her bright, brown eyes hid many tears. She lived alone in a modest, decent, and clean house. She'd lost her husband in a freak work accident—he'd been plastering the walls of a tall building when he'd fallen from the ladder. At the time, Lucy was an unemployed housewife, and was suddenly left all alone to look after her only son, Roger, who was just ten-years-old. Struggling with the little money she received from her widow's pension, Lucy was forced to work two jobs to pay the bills and provide an education for her son, whom she raised to the best of her ability. Roger was such a sweet little boy until he mingled with the troubled, older kids at school. And, tragically, the hard-working single mother ended up losing her only child to the lure of drugs.

Lucy had known at the time those older kids were bad news and tried in vain to put a stop to Roger hanging out with them. So many times she tried to get him on the right path of life, but all her attempts—even with the help of the city's Youth Department—proved unsuccessful. Roger ran away from home countless times to be with his drug-addicted friends, only to be brought back home by the police.

Finally, Roger ran away from home at the age of sixteen and never came back. Lucy only saw him now and again, and he did come by to say *hello* and introduce his new girlfriend, Emma. Emma, as Lucy found out later, was also a runaway. Roger was eighteen years of age by then, and Emma was seventeen and pregnant with Laura. Just two years after that, nineteen-year-old Emma gave birth to Libby. When the girls were born, Laura was the spitting image of her mother and Libby looked more like her father.

The heartbroken grandmother kept a watchful eye on her granddaughters. On many occasions she reported their neglect to Social Security and offered to take Laura and Libby under her protective wing. She would call by their house to bring food and little gifts, and wanted nothing more than to remove them from that terrible, toxic environment. Lucy wanted to ensure her granddaughters wouldn't follow their parent's path, but Roger and Emma never allowed her to take them as they knew they'd lose their social security benefits—the only thing they *really* cared about.

Roger was a tall, slim man with dark, curly hair. Dark, weary circles surrounded his once-inquisitive, deep, brown eyes and their pupils were always constricted. He'd learned to hide the needle marks on his arms under the long-sleeved shirts he always wore, even on the warmest summer days; Roger constantly looked sick from his toxic substance dependency and alcohol abuse.

Emma had been an incredibly beautiful, statuesque young woman before she lost her vivacity to drugs. The dilated pupils of her eyes soon gave way to the red—once such a stunning green—that surrounded them, and her naturally trim frame suffered such dramatic weight loss over the years of drug use that Lucy feared the girl was anorexic.

Many were the times Laura and Libby had to help their nauseous mother to the toilet to vomit; her slurred speech would become so incoherent they couldn't even begin to understand her. It had been manageable at one time for the two young sisters, but over the two years before they were removed from their home, the situation had worsened—once Emma and Roger moved from using marijuana and smack cocaine to the heavy, especially nasty drugs that were systematically destroying their lives. With those, and as their personal hygiene declined, they more often resembled a pair of zombies.

Libby and Laura would often find themselves falling asleep on the grimy old sofas that occupied the mess of the living room of their small, two-bedroom apartment. The floor was always strewn with broken cigarettes with their filters removed, bent, blackened spoons, and candles—all clear indications of their parent's addiction. With every possible penny spent on drugs, money problems were a constant—there was rarely ever any food, treats, or comforts to be had at home.

So, one can only imagine the relief and happiness in Lucy's heart as tears of joy rolled down her face when the social worker knocked on her door with her granddaughters—her two little treasures. Finally, she had full custody of Laura and Libby!

Before then, school had not been the children's priority. They'd never been able to concentrate enough to do well in their studies because of their tragic family circumstances. However, their sweet grandmother guided them by example, instilled good values, and encouraged the girls. "You can be whatever you want to be. Fight for it! It doesn't matter where you come from... but where you go!" she would tell them as she packed them off to school each day. And slowly but surely, with care and love, Lucy's granddaughters began to turn themselves around.

Laura was smart enough to know her only escape from poverty, to better herself, was through education. This was now possible because the days of roaming the streets looking for food were finally behind her—her grandmother *always* had food on the table.

Changing their attitudes, the girls made school their number one priority and both applied themselves to excel—each in their own way. Laura dreamed of becoming a lawyer and knew her only chance to achieve that goal was by winning a university scholarship. In order to achieve that she also knew she had to work *really* hard. The only hobby Laura had time for was sketching on the weekends—it helped her relax and distracted her mind from the rigorous school duties and daily routines.

Libby, being the more outgoing of the two, loved playing with her friends in the neighborhood or, if she chose to stay home, reading.

Laura became a bright, outstanding student and even cut two years off finishing the four-year high school curriculum. She was especially strong-minded and refused to let her circumstances keep her down. Laura developed a passion for helping others and had long decided she wanted to be a lawyer to help fight for the rights of the less fortunate and vulnerable populations in the world. *No child should suffer what Libby and I went through*, she thought, *everybody deserves a chance in life.*

The hard work Laura did in her younger years paid off, and all her aspirations came to fruition as she was awarded a full scholarship from the University of Harvard in Cambridge, Massachusetts.

A new chapter in Laura's life was about to start—with many challenges and battles to overcome!

Chapter 2

Laura moved away from home in Patterson, a middle class Louisiana community, to Massachusetts to attend university. As she walked through the wide, imposing gate, she looked around and took a big, deep breath. *Whoa! Here I am! This is another world completely!*

She couldn't help but be impressed by the beauty of the campus and the myriad awesome spaces to explore between the academic buildings, libraries, and beautiful hidden gem gardens.

Laura was taken to her campus faculty and handed the keys to her dorm room. She was to share with another girl, Claire, who was waiting for her in their room.

"Hi, I'm Laura, nice to meet you," Laura introduced herself politely.

"Hi, Laura, I'm Claire. Nice to meet you, too!" her new roommate replied. "I just arrived yesterday, so we have a lot to explore. Come, I'll show you around."

"Thank you!" Laura smiled.

Each girl had a small, single room with a bed, a single wardrobe, a desk, and a chair. Both rooms had a window with a nice view of the garden. A shared toilet, bathroom, and a sitting area with a sofa and TV completed their cozy accommodation.

Laura was delighted with the facilities—it was all very much nicer and larger than she was accustomed to—and with Claire, the friendly French national, it felt a like home.

During school holidays, Laura would visit her grandmother and sister. Libby was, of course, still in high school.

Laura soon met Robert, and he became her first proper boyfriend. Even though he was cute, attentive, and charming, the relationship wasn't to last. Laura had to focus on her studies and didn't seem to have time for him. Eventually, they broke up and Robert quickly moved on to a new girlfriend. Laura hadn't really been *in love* with Robert, but she did like him a lot—so much so her heart would miss a beat when she saw Robert so soon afterward with his new girlfriend.

"Gosh, that was *fast*!" she said to Claire.

"Yes, Laura, but you didn't really spend much time with him!" her friend replied. "Remember how he was always complaining about that? You actually spent more of your free time with me instead of poor Robert!"

"I guess you're right, Claire," Laura was forced to admit. "Oh, well, I do wish Robert well. I just didn't expect him to find a new girlfriend so fast, that's all."

"He is actually quite cute, Laura, and he *really* loved you! Poor thing—it's a pity you pushed him away!"

"Maybe he's not the one for me." Laura sighed. "Or should I say, I'm just not ready to have a boyfriend? My focus has to be on my studies! But, yes, he's an awesome boy—I really do hope he finds the one for him!"

Looking back, Laura recalled just how many times she'd left poor Robert standing; she knew in her heart Claire was right. *I never had much time for him at all,* she thought to herself.

Moving quickly away from her sad thoughts, Laura immersed herself in her daily life on campus and made studies her first priority.

She and Claire both enjoyed swimming very much. And so, early every morning they would head out for a rigorous half-hour at Harvard's renowned sports facility. It was a perfect way to start the day and help them concentrate. On the weekends, after home duties and folding the laundry, they would drop into their favorite cafe for a relaxing chat, and occasionally they'd catch a movie at the local cinema.

With much hard work and dedication, Laura graduated with a degree in International Law—with honors and distinctions. In the final academic year of her university degree program, Laura applied for an internship with the Office of Legal Affairs (OLA), which was managed by the United Nations Office for Human Resources Management. She fulfilled all the requirements and, much to her delight, Laura was granted admission to the highly competitive OLA program. As an intern, all of her costs, arrangements for travel, visas, accommodation, and living expenses came under the full responsibility of Harvard University! Laura was also incredibly jubilant to be deployed to Tanzania for her internship.

She said her sad goodbyes to Claire on the day she left; she was truly going to miss her roommate, who still had a year of studying to go with her marine biology degree.

"Good luck, Laura." Claire fought to hold back the tears. "All the very best. I'll miss you."

"Thank you, Claire. We have each other's numbers, we'll keep in touch," Laura reassured. "Good luck with your studies too!"

In Africa, Laura took part in as many volunteer projects in hospitals, refugee camps, and children's workshops as she possibly could. Under the supervision of the OLA, Laura undertook tasks in projects that give her a unique insight into a UN diplomat's work, along with the functioning of the United Nations itself.

The whole experience was incredibly enriching and made a big impact on Laura. The powerful survival stories, along with the physical and mental scars carried by the people she worked with, particularly in the refugee camps, were unbelievably touching.

She couldn't help but be shocked by the severity of the harsh situations of those she encountered in Tanzania, which all the more made her determined to make a difference

The Camps in Tanzania were overcrowded and totally dependent on the humanitarian aid programs. The refugees had fled from neighboring countries to escape the horrific genocides in Burundi and Rwanda. Those poor people had lost everything, including family members. Many more were left mutilated, and children had become separated from their parents or, worse still, left as orphans. Yet, on the brink of so many psychological traumas they faced, the refugees found the strength and means to support one another in those adverse circumstances.

Of course, registering the children's and parent's identities, along with trying to reunite them, were absolute priorities, as was responding to the demands of the growing refugee crisis—basic health programs and widespread immunization were rapidly instigated.

Laura joined forces with her colleagues at the mission to implement humanitarian programs to improve the good health and wellbeing of people in poor communities—in particular, children who were vulnerable to infections due to lack of hygiene and adequate access to safe drinking water and sanitation. She also provided information to the local Radio Community Programs to bring issues to the forefront, as well as the much-needed aid programs and health education concerns. By raising such awareness, the impact of the UN's work was very real and visible.

While her own experiences as a child were not quite so dramatic, Laura felt she could relate to the suffering of the children she was trying to help; it made her feel good to be making such a difference to their lives.

All the work and experience abroad also helped Laura improve her public speaking and negotiation skills, and provide her with better knowledge about global affairs—as well as enhancing her research and policy analysis capabilities.

The work was both challenging and illuminating, and Laura was absolutely thrilled with the amazing work of the United Nations. She took full advantage of every opportunity the OLA offered, which enabled her to experience different international fields.

Laura's tireless passion and commitment didn't go unnoticed. After six months, when she'd completed the internship, she was offered a job by the Equality and Human Rights Commission in Manchester, England. Naturally, Laura grabbed the opportunity with both hands and began her job there as Assistant Director for Programs. It was there she met Frank Webley, the Deputy Executive Director for Programs.

Handsome, ten years older than Laura, Frank had recently separated from his wife and two teenage boys. A youthful, good-looking multi-millionaire, Frank was hard-working and dedicated to his UN work. His late father, Robert Webley, had been a well-known tycoon in the finance and business world who had specialized in financial investment risk-assessment. Despite his father's wishes, Frank's passion had never been for the financial world. Frank's degree and expertise was law—he specialized in international law, and gained extensive experience representing his country in countless bilateral and multilateral forums. Despite disappointing his father, as the only son, Frank had inherited the enormous wealth Robert Webley had accumulated throughout his illustrious career.

Frank's powerful, charming presence could easily fill a room. He also had a wonderful sense of humor and never failed to make Laura laugh. Laura was endlessly impressed by his powerful personality and hard work, and she learned a tremendous amount as she accompanied him everywhere on official UN business.

There were many times Laura would stay late in the office to work with Frank. It was a true privilege to have the opportunity to learn so much about international law, humanitarian aid, refugees, terrorism, poverty, promoting the rights of the most vulnerable people in society, and the issues affecting humanity as a whole.

Somewhat inevitably, Laura and Frank grew ever closer as they enjoyed innumerable dinners out and free time together. And, before too long, they had become romantically involved.

Laura was committed and passionate about her work. She learned it both out in the field and with Frank. She travelled frequently with him, and he gave her a unique insight into the complexity of UN programs. The Commission Body itself was mainly responsible for enforcing equality, freedom, and the basic human rights of every human being in the world—in a nutshell, eliminating all types of discrimination. It was all such a steep learning curve for Laura, but it did give her the opportunities she needed to open her horizons and develop a vast and outstanding curriculum.

Just two years on, and she was promoted to Director of Programs. Slowly but steadily, Laura became an incredibly well known Human Rights Lawyer, as well as a respected and recognized face at all major U.N. conferences, seminars, and human rights councils.

Of course, Laura's work took her all over the globe, which meant being away from her beloved Frank. On one of Laura's homecomings, Frank was waiting for her at the airport with a huge, stunningly beautiful bunch of flowers. He escorted her to an awaiting limousine and had her close her eyes for the entire journey…

When they finally arrived at their destination, Frank told her to keep her eyes closed tight as he opened the car door and helped her out. "Don't open your eyes yet… it's a surprise. You can only open them when I tell you," he said with a playfully mysterious tone.

"A surprise? Hmm… does it have anything to do with the properties we've been looking at? Laura joked.

"Well, you can try guessing, my darling, but it wouldn't be much of a surprise if I told you." Frank laughed. "Just be patient—and keep your eyes closed; we're almost there…"

Smiling, Laura allowed Frank to guide her—holding his hand tightly across the short distance until they came to a stop. She had a vague idea as to his surprise, but didn't want to spoil the moment for him.

"Don't open your eyes until I tell you!"

"Okay, okay!" Laura couldn't help giggling. "I can't wait!" She heard a door swing open. Frank led her into a room and closed the door behind them.

"You can open your eyes… *now!*" Frank smiled at Laura as she blinked against the suddenness of the light. "Welcome to our new home!"

Laura looked around with her hand clasped over her heart. "Seriously?" She gazed into Frank's stunning eyes. "This is beautiful! It's the one I loved the most!"

The house, nestled in the most respectable suburb of Didsbury, Great Manchester, was an absolute gem. Laura immediately fell in love with the quiet placidity of the landscape, which was surrounded by a lovely garden and cozy backyard. The house itself was not far from the River Mersey and overlooked the beauty and serenity of a golf course. Laura could picture she and Frank savoring a cup of tea on the stone seat in the middle of the backyard as they watched the golfers and the countless visiting birds.

The two-story house of five bedrooms had gloriously high ceilings and long, high French windows at both front and back, which overlooked the garden. Beautifully outsized ceramic marble tiles covered the floor from the entry hall to the media room, and beyond that sat a French door, which opened onto an ample double living room with bare timber floors. There, a massive stone fireplace sat between two large windows, and at the center of the room's timber, cathedral-style ceiling there hung a stunning crystal chandelier. The view of the backyard from the living room and the adjacent, elegant dining room was peaceful and breathtaking all at the same time.

The rear deck was vibrant with the sound of cascading water from the rock waterfall of the swimming pool. The pool was a sumptuous aqua blue color and had an atmosphere of tranquility that Laura immediately fell in love with.

"I don't know what to say!" Laura said to Frank as she gazed in amazement around the house.

"Just say *yes*," he replied.

"Yes to what?"

Frank dropped to one knee. With a sheepish grin, he plucked a little box from his pocket and opened it. From within, a stunning, fat diamond shone at Laura. "Would you do me the honor of marrying me?" he asked.

Without hesitation and with a tear of joy in her eye, Laura gave her answer, "Yes, yes, and *yes*! I love you, darling!"

In attendance at the wedding, of course, was Laura's grandmother—who was now the grand old age of eighty-two. She lived with Libby, now a high school English teacher who had married her high school sweetheart, Mark. He was a skilled mathematician and a teacher at the same school.

Frank's sons, Sam and Michael, his and Laura's colleagues from work, and their closest friends were all at the memorable, elegant ceremony at the iconic, historic Manchester Hall.

Laura had organized her wedding with the same diligence as everything in her life. Everything was meticulous and her personal touch in every detail made everything all the more special and glamorous! The wedding venue itself looked unbelievably elegant. There were glittering crystal chandeliers, exquisitely designed silver cutlery, and white blossoms; soft pink and lavender colored flowers mixed with tiny dry fruits adorned each table.

And as for the bride herself, Laura looked impossibly beautiful in a Ruff & Russell white wedding gown. It was complemented with a delicate crystal necklace, earrings, and bracelets, along with a headpiece adorned with tiny white roses. Laura drew gasps of admiration as she made her entrance through the dreamy flower arch in the gardens, holding bouquet of white and soft pink roses. She was given away by her brother-in-law, Mark, who looked quite dashing in his Yves Saint Laurent tuxedo.

It was an absolutely perfect day; the wedding reception was chick, stylish, and most luxurious. As the sun set and night fell, the twinkling starlight exuded a rare brilliance, which made their first dance truly magical.

Laura and Frank enjoyed their honeymoon in the sunshine and exotic scenery of the Caribbean island paradise of St. Lucia. They swam in the crystal blue sea and sunbathed on the gorgeous sandy beaches. They explored the lush, green mountains and had romantic evenings watching the sunset from the private balcony of their traditional bungalow—their love was certainly well celebrated.

Then, it was back to work after the honeymoon. Life soon resumed its normal course.

Both incredibly career-oriented, Frank and Laura loved their work and took their responsibilities very seriously. Indeed, even in their free time together, there was no end to the professional issues they discussed well into the late hours of the night.

Laura's dreams of having children were put on hold. At this stage of her life, her career was everything. And besides, Frank was already a parent—they made sure to see his two boys on a regular basis. However, Frank was more than happy to have children with Laura some day— he knew just how much she longed to be a mother. He also knew she would give work a pause and slow down when she was ready.

Fully committed and involved in their work, Laura and Frank's traveling became ever more frequent—with the two, unfortunately, quite literally flying in different directions. Three years had flown by and they saw less and less of each other. But wherever in the world they found themselves, they would always call each other to say goodnight.

Another year into the marriage and their hectic lifestyle, along with the travel essential to their careers, kept them apart. Slowly, surely, the spark and emotion of their relationship began to wane.

By then, Frank didn't always call to say goodnight as he once had, and often times he didn't pick up the phone or return his wife's calls.

"I called you three times and left messages," Laura would complain. "You didn't bother to call me back!"

"Sorry, darling, I was in a meeting," Frank explained. "It finished too late to return your call—I thought you'd be asleep!"

"No, I wasn't. I was waiting for you to call me."

"I'm sorry, darling, I really did finish late."

Laura put the blame upon the intensity of their work and the extended periods of time they spent apart. And so, unhappy with the path their marriage was taking, Laura determined to change things—beginning with slowing down at work and reducing the traveling that kept them apart.

Flying back home from an overseas trip a day early, Laura planned to surprise her husband by treating him to dinner at their favorite Thai restaurant to enjoy the food they both loved. Laura was excited to tell Frank of her plans to slow down and suggest a holiday break—maybe even a Mediterranean cruise. She also wanted to talk to him about children—she was ready to be a mother!

It was late in the afternoon when Laura got home from the airport. She took a shower and then squeezed into a chic, black mini dress that showed off her killer legs, which she complimented with elegant, patent leather black high heels. She made the final touches with red lipstick—as always—the gorgeous pendant earrings Frank had given her on her last birthday, and wore her bouncing, shiny, strawberry blond locks down one side of her neck. Laura looked absolutely perfect! Scrutinizing every last detail from head to toe, Laura took a good, long look at herself in the mirror. *That'll do nicely,* she thought to herself, and she left happy!

Anxious to see her husband, Laura drove to the Manchester Arndale Centre, which housed his office. She was delighted to see his car parked there.

She had planned to get to Frank's office before closing time but the busy city center traffic delayed her. So, it was a little after hours when she finally got there. Laura knew Frank was incredibly busy—it wasn't at all unusual for him to work late at the office. Taking the elevator, Laura stopped at the fifth floor with her heart pounding hard in her chest.

Opening the front door, she walked by the empty reception desk and saw the lights were on in Frank's office. She gently knocked upon the office door before opening it with a big smile on her face—little did she know the devastating surprise that was in store for her!

In an instant, the smile vanished from Laura's face. There was Frank, caught with his pants down—*literally*—having sex on his desk with his new assistant! The girl, Gina, was a cute redhead around the same age as Laura.

"Oh my God!" Laura cried out. Shaking, she covered her mouth with one hand as her eyes filled with water and fat teardrops rolled down her face.

"Laura!" Frank was taken completely by surprise at his wife's unexpected visit. He pushed Gina away and ran after Laura.

Laura turned her back, ran from her husband's office, and took the elevator to the car park.

"Laura! Laura! Please stop!" Frank pleaded. *"We can talk about this!"*

Laura ignored him and ran to her car as fast as she could in four-inch heels. Jumping in, she started up the car and, with the tires squealing, she sped away. In her rearview mirror, she could see Frank standing in the middle of the car park with his hands over his head in despair.

"SHIT!" he shouted after her. *"SHIT! DAMN IT!"* Frank cried out his frustration.

It was Friday night and the traffic was heavy with the usual weekend crowds heading out for a night of entertainment. Laura was distraught and stuck in it all; she was still trembling with shock and her heart was in knots over her husband's shocking betrayal.

She didn't want to go home—it somehow didn't feel like *home* anymore. Frank called her cell phone incessantly, which she refused to pick up. Annoyed, she FINALLY turned the thing off and threw it on the floor of her car. She drove to the nearby Hilton Hotel, left her car at the front for the valet parking, and marched straight to the reception desk. There, Laura booked a suite for the week—she knew she wouldn't be going back home any time soon. Plus, she needed some time to decide what to do next.

Needless to say, poor Laura spent the night numb, her face wet with tears, as she questioned the very meaning of her existence. Memories of her stolen childhood blazed through her memory—she'd fought so hard to escape the poverty caused by her parents' addictions. Only a year after she and her sister were given into their grandmother's care, their parents had both died in a car crash. The car was driven by Jose, one of their druggie friends— the driver and passengers were all drunk and high at the time. That tragedy, on top of her deprived upbringing, had marked Laura's young years only to come to this. Just what was her destiny?

Suffering! That's it, she thought to herself. Laura felt as if the universe itself was conspiring against her.

Throughout her entire life, Laura had struggled with her emotions. And, more often than not, her depressive thoughts would take the best of her. She'd spent her younger years in hardship trying to escape the ineffable labyrinth of her sad life and dreaming of how awesome it would be to achieve what she'd actually achieved. She had been so happy with her life with Frank—she'd felt on the top of the world!

But... the irony of a cruel destiny!

Happiness had eluded Laura once more. Her world had fallen apart and here she was again. Lost, she felt as if all her hard work had led to the lonely life she was now facing. Her only solace came in the form of wise words from her younger sister, Libby—the first person she had called that terrible night—*"You have always been a strong and resilient person, Laura. You feel broken now, but it will pass—you'll see! Remember, everything happens for a reason, and each step of the way leads to another path. You have come a long way. You thought you had reached your peak. But you didn't, Laura! Have faith! Your strength will inspire you! Your peak is still to come! You'll see..."*

Laura found out from her secretary, Nancy that Frank's affair had been going on for three months. It had begun shortly after Gina started working as Frank's new assistant. Apparently, everyone in the office *knew*. Even though her colleagues had frowned upon their flirting ways, they'd said nothing to Laura. That hurt her almost as much as her husband's betrayal.

Thinking back, Laura recalled noticing that Frank would receive strange phone calls at home. Sometimes he would whisper and walk out into the garden to talk out of her earshot. Laura had dismissed her suspicions as silly at the time. She'd ask him who it was, and he'd say, "Oh, just work, my darling—nothing major!" He'd then excuse himself for walking out by blaming it on bad cell phone reception inside the house. At work, he and Gina had sure covered up their affair incredibly well—in her presence at least—as Laura hadn't noticed anything suspicious there at all.

More than the involvement of her husband with another woman, it was the betrayal of trust that came as a painful revelation for Laura. Everything had changed now, and there wasn't any way back. Not for Laura! The tears, rage, and despair that Frank had brought to her heart would be impossible to ignore—that much she knew for certain. Her trust in him had been irreparably damaged. And with the trust gone, Laura's marriage was over.

Two days later, making sure Frank was away on a work trip, Laura finally made the move to return home to pick up her clothes, shoes, and personal items.

A chill coursed through Laura's veins as she walked into the house. Questions buzzed through her racing mind: *Has* she *been here? Did Frank bring Gina to our house... to our bed?!* Her nerves jangled at the tormenting thoughts.

With no more delay, Laura took a quick look around—the last one—at the home that just wasn't hers anymore. She couldn't bear the thought of living in a house full of memories—that would only hurt her heart even more. She needed fresh air to breathe because the air in the house was polluted, heavy, and tense.

With her husband's unforgivable deceit ripping her heart apart, Laura left her keys on the kitchen bench top and closed the door behind her.

Laura resigned from her office. She simply couldn't bear to work there any longer with Frank, Gina, and even her colleagues as the atmosphere there had become quite toxic.

Although she had not made any immediate decisions, Laura knew she had to change her life. She considered joining Libby and Mark on their holiday in Portugal; Libby had booked a stopover in Manchester to spend a few days with Laura and Frank before flying on to Lisbon. Things had changed now, of course. Laura and Frank's sudden separation caught Libby and Mark completely by surprise. However, Laura insisted she didn't want it to interfere with their travel arrangements—it would be expensive to make new ones. So, instead of staying at Laura and

Frank's home as planned, they booked a room in the hotel Laura was using as her temporary home; things were easier that way. And besides, Libby wanted time to convince Laura to join her and Mark on their holiday.

Not wishing to spoil her sister's holiday with her emotions all over the place, Laura had declined at first. But Libby, never one to give up, refused take no for an answer. She had then threatened to kidnap Laura and drag her along with them if necessary!

Laura knew she needed Libby's company, as her sister's spark was always good for her. Despite following different paths and the distance separating them, Laura and Libby had maintained a strong bond over the years.

While Libby was the younger of the two sisters, she definitely was the more strong-minded. Bright and imaginative, she was always the one to break the rules in her younger days. Laura found it hard to believe that, given Libby's devil-may-care attitude and free spirit, she had secured a job at one of the most prestigious private Colleges of Louisiana. As determined as Laura, Libby had applied herself throughout her education to fulfill her dream of becoming a teacher. Both girls, in their own ways, had become remarkable young women.

And so, there was Libby once again. Just as when they'd been small children on the brink of starvation, she was ready to take the reins and bring her sister back from the depths of depression.

Feelings of desperate loneliness dragged Laura down during the days. Unable to sleep and eat properly, debilitating inertia gripped her psyche. One by one, Laura shut out her friends and lost all motivation and zest for life. But she couldn't shut out Libby—her younger sibling just wouldn't give up on her sister… or take *no* for an answer.

Laura's birthday came five days after the shocking episode, and Laura had to wait another week for the end of the school term before Libby could join her. So, poor Laura spent her birthday alone in the hotel.

Waking up early on the warm Friday morning of her birthday, Laura decided to make an effort and go for a walk around a nearby park and a swim in the hotel swimming pool. Sad and alone, she returned to her room to find a small, round, white cake with *Happy Birthday* written neatly in pink icing on its top. Next to it sat a bottle of champagne in a silver ice bucket. It was a nice, personal touch on behalf of the hotel, which had a policy of marking a guest's birthday. A card from the hotel wished her a happy birthday; it was placed next to the cake on a small table set for one. The single champagne glass brought to Laura's mind the realization that she was so desperately lonely. Far more than she'd ever felt before in her entire life.

Darkness reached out from Laura's shattered heart as a blind fury took over her. Grabbing the champagne glass, she threw it with all her might into the small rubbish bin. There, just like her heart, it broke into a thousand pieces.

As hard as she tried, Laura just couldn't get the image of her husband having sex with another woman out of her head. Laura usually only drank on social occasions—one or two glasses at the most—but that night she decided to take on the entire bottle of champagne.

With trembling hands, she untwisted the wire from around the cork and attempted to open the bottle. The cork refused to come out. Frustrated, Laura shook the bottle so hard the cork eventually popped itself! Along with the cork, expensive champagne exploded all over Laura and showered her clothes, the furniture, the walls, and the carpet.

"You're not going to win, you stupid, stupid bottle!" she shouted in victory. With the champagne glass shattered and useless in the bin, Laura brought the bottle to her mouth and gulped from it like a man rescued from the desert.

Sitting there like a dripping wet, disheveled rag doll in the middle of the hotel's king sized bed, Laura could see herself at the mirror; she looked so funny with her hair dripping with champagne and clinging to her nose—like a wild cat that had just fallen into a bucket of water! Sadly, Laura was unable to find the humor in her sorry situation, so she drained the bottle and cried herself to sleep. It was quite bewildering and somewhat alien for Laura to feel so broken and off balance; she kept on asking herself over and over, *What happened to me? What happened to* us?

Libby and Mark finally arrived in Manchester. At her sister's insistence, and left without any choice in the matter, Laura was to join them on their holiday in Portugal. More than ever, she needed Libby's strength, but also the tender, loving side she knew so well.

So, early the next morning, Laura, Libby, and Mark went together by taxi from the hotel to the airport. From there, they traveled straight to Lisbon with TAP, the Portuguese Airline. Libby and Mark had deliberately cut short their stay in Manchester, as Libby just wanted to take her poor sister away from that city and all its bitter memories.

Chapter 3

Laura booked a room at the same Lisbon hotel as Libby and Mark—the Lapa Palace. It was a classic, nineteenth-century mansion located in the heart of the capital city. Losing no time, after checking in and leaving their luggage in their rooms, the three strolled through the charming streets of that friendly city, which boasted an incredibly cosmopolitan population. They made their way to downtown Baixa Pombalina, Rossio, and Restauradores—the latter a potential candidate to become a World Heritage Site. It had been rebuilt by the famous Marques de Pombal following the devastating 1975 earthquake that had destroyed so much of the city.

Of course, like most women, Laura and Libby loved shopping! In the beating heart of the city center, they visited the luxury shops at *Avenida da Liberdade*. Enraptured by the sheer elegance of the exclusive designs the shops carried, Laura and Libby lost their minds in an over-the-top shopping frenzy—much to the amusement and delight of the commissioned staff!

Mark waited patiently for them at a nearby café. He enjoyed the quiet time and read *The Portugal News*—the country's national newspaper, which was printed in English and covered all the major news for the almost fifty thousand Brits living in Portugal. Every now and then he'd glance at his watch.

When Laura and Libby did finally arrive, they were weighed down with shopping bags.

"Next time, I'll stay at the hotel pool instead of being your pack-horse." He joked as they handed him their haul to carry to the car.

The trio then made their way to *Casa da Cerveja*—'Beer House'—where they visited the *Museu da Cerveja*—'Beer Museum'—to savor the excellent quality *Cerveja*, which was served in original glasses. The waterside location was simply outstanding, and although the inside seating area was spectacular, they chose to sit outside—they'd hit lucky and managed to find the only available table on the packed terrace with views of the Tagus River. From the mouthwatering Portuguese menu, they chose the *bacalhau*—the traditional national dish comprising the most mouthwatering codfish. They ate, drank, and talked as they enjoyed one another's company and soaked up the relaxing atmosphere.

After a long day out, Laura and Libby headed back to the hotel to rest up before dinner. Exhausted, Laura lay in her bed, closed her eyes, and finally managed to sleep well for the first time in a long time.

She was awoken by a call from her sister.

"Just checking if you're awake, Laura!" Libby trilled. "You need to be ready for dinner!"

"Okay," Laura groaned, "I'll have a shower and meet you both at the reception desk in one hour."

"That's perfect! We'll be ready!"

That night they had dinner in the famous *Clube do Fado* in the old picturesque town of Alfama, which lay just outside Lisbon. There, they enjoyed the very best Portuguese traditional cooking and the sounds of a Portuguese Guitar with Fado voices—Fado is exquisitely expressive in nature, and profoundly melancholy. It reflects life's hard realities, lost loves, longings, and other torments of the heart.

The atmosphere of the Fado House was delightful and calming. Although the sisters couldn't understand the lyrics, the songs and the Portuguese guitar—accompanied by such a profoundly intense voice of heartfelt emotion—could entrance any heart longing for a lost love. The lyrics captured a difficult, sad life and brought Laura to tears; while she didn't understand a word of what they were singing, the whole ambiance perfectly mirrored her melancholy state of mind. Nevertheless, it was a magical night and a truly fantastic experience.

During their time in Portugal, Laura and Libby enjoyed much more of Lisbon's rich culture. They visited castles, churches, and the most amazing monuments—many of which were the result of Celtic, Germanic, Moorish, and Jewish influences upon the predominantly Roman Catholic country.

After a week in Lisbon, they left the hotel early in the morning and headed to Sintra, which was a thirty-minute drive away. Laura had booked all three of them in the Seteais Palace—an absolutely beautiful neoclassical palace that had been converted into a luxury hotel.

Laura marveled at the picturesque Portuguese town on the hills of the *Serra de Sintra*. It boasted exquisite palaces, luxuriant mansions, and the most amazingly designed decorative gardens. The place was truly a rare slice of Portuguese history, which boasted links to the nobility and elite of the country.

Sintra's town center was incredibly charming and inviting. Its pretty cobbled streets, lined with traditional houses, shops, and cafes, were spread across the steep hills. Everything was centered on the Gothic-styled National Palace, which, in itself, had so much to offer.

The beautiful scenery of the wonderful town and its fascinating historic buildings had made Sintra a renowned tourist destination. Sintra also offered scenic walks through the rainforest and hidden lakes of *Parque da Pena* that surround the nineteenth century *Palácio da Pena,* which was of the Romanticism style of architecture and stood apart in the charming town.

Laura was particularly impressed with the palace's exterior. It had the most exquisite statues of mythological creatures adorning its walls, which, in turn, were painted and tiled with the most vivid colors.

The village of Sintra, with more than two hundred years of history, was one of the most beautiful places in the world; in 1995 it was claimed by UNESCO as World Heritage. The sites of the restored, historic buildings, decadent mansions, and ancient castle ruins were sign-posted throughout the town—each and every one well worth seeking out.

The busy city center offered a vibrant ambience with pottery studios, art galleries, and cozy coffee shops. The trio enjoyed a pleasant outdoor lunch menu after a full morning of sightseeing.

Sadly, Libby and Mark's holiday came to an end and it came time to return to Louisiana and to work. They invited Laura to return home with them until she recovered from the emotional consequences of her recent experience with Frank.

Graciously refusing the kind invitation, Laura decided to stay in Sintra. Having fallen in love with the place, she wanted to explore it further.

"What are you going to do here all by yourself?" a concerned Libby asked.

"I don't know," Laura replied with a smile. "I love it here— I'll stay for a while to relax before deciding. I'm not in a hurry to go anywhere."

Libby relaxed. She was confident Laura was on the way to recovering from her deep depression. She knew the long walks she'd shared with her sister had helped her a great deal. Mark had been wonderfully understanding, and had given the sisters the crucial space they'd needed to be alone with one another,

Their long conversations, while walking through the beautiful gardens and forests of Sintra, had helped Laura to calm her mind. Libby's strength, care, and love had provided the sense of trust and comfort she so much needed to begin to rebuild her shattered life.

The sisters said their tearful goodbyes as Libby and Mark returned to their hotel in Lisbon to spend one final night before traveling back home early the following the morning.

After her sister's departure, Laura lived at the hotel until she found what she was looking for: her own house. She had no desire to do anything other than take a good, long break to dedicate time to herself and the simple things in life she'd never had the time for before. She loved nature, long walks, reading, and, above all, she rediscovered her passion for painting.

Laura didn't crave an extravagant lifestyle, and since she'd made a comfortable fortune with her hard, well-paid work, she was comfortably off. She'd also made some smart, successful investments, which provided a decent income.

For now, staying in the beautiful town she had fallen in love with—Sintra—was all Laura wanted! *What's the best place to be but right here?* she asked herself

Every day, Laura took some time to stroll around the town center. She would frequent the real estate offices as she looked for something rustic and picturesque in the country. The real estate agent, Mr. Manuel, drove Laura around to view properties for sale, but so far she hadn't really found that extra-special one to call home.

On their way back from yet another viewing, a little way along a narrow road on top of a hill, Laura noticed a *For Sale* sign hanging on the front wall of a manor house. She loved the area and the position of the house, and was eager to find out more. "How about this one?" she asked Mr. Manuel.

"Oh, that one is in very poor condition." Manuel slowed the car down to a stop just in front of the gate. "I don't think you'd like it at all. It's been abandoned for a very long time. The heirs have been in conflict, and the house has been on the market for almost ten years. I really don't think that's the house for you, miss."

Surrounded by over a hectare of overgrown grass and unruly undergrowth, the house, built in 1930, was uninhabited and crumbling after many years of neglect; as far as Laura could see, there was flaking paint peeling from *every* wall. Yet, there was something about the house that appealed to Laura. "I want to see it." She was quite firm on the matter.

"Okay, miss, I can show you around. But be aware… it's even far worse inside than you think!"

Undeterred, Laura pressed the man, "When can we do it?"

"Now, if you wish. I just have to pick up the keys from my office.

"What are we waiting for?"

Without further ado, Manuel drove straight to the office to pick up the keys. In just twenty minutes, he was turning back into that narrow road on the top of the hill. Shortly after that, he parked in front of the tall, black iron gate that secured the entrance to the old manor house.

"Here we are again." Laura could barely conceal her excitement.

"Yes," he replied. "You can't really see much of the house from the road—it's mostly hidden behind all those trees and grass. I did warn you it would be much worse than you thought!" He smiled at Laura. "Please, wait in the car. I'll open the gate and drive us up to the house—it's a bit too far to walk."

Climbing back into the car, Manuel drove about two hundred meters down the bumpy dirt road that ran between the tall, dense pine trees and high grass until Laura finally caught sight of the house in the middle of the spacious grounds.

Manuel got out of the car and Laura followed suit. She then trailed the realtor through the long, straggly weeds, which all but concealed the front door, to get to the large front portico.

Aged and battered by the elements, the rustic home was indeed in need of great care and attention. The exterior wall paint was completely gone, most of the windows were broken, and at its front, what had once certainly been a beautiful garden was smothered by dead branches and elongated weeds.

"I'm very sorry, miss," Manuel apologized profusely. "The house has been abandoned for so long... The original owners died decades ago and the heirs of the property live in Brazil. They don't want to spend any money with the house being as old as it is—not even to treat the grass and weeds. They just want to sell it as it is."

"That's a pity," Laura replied. "But I can see its beauty through the mess."

"Then let's go in!" Manuel's mood picked up at his client's strange enthusiasm. He unlocked the solid wood door. The rusty hinges screamed out loud as it swung open.

The generously sized entry hall, resplendent with typical Portuguese dark red floor tiles, opened out into a large living area, which showcased the beautifully old timber floors. The elaborate, high ceilings with their ornate detailing were still very much intact. In the middle of the expansive room sat an antique, black iron fireplace, and on either side of that, there were two broken picture windows, which offered dramatic and uninterrupted views over *Serra de Sintra Palácio* and *Park de Monserrato*.

In one corner there were burned timbers and ashes scattered across the floor. "What happened there?" Laura wanted to know.

"There was a fire last summer," Manuel explained. "An abandoned house is always a magnet to drug addicts and bad people. I suggested that the owners take on a permanent security guard, but they refused to pay."

Laura tagged along as the agent went from room to dilapidated room. As she did so, she inspected every square inch of that 1930's building, which was simply crying out to be restored.

The manor house was divided into three floors with a huge connecting spiral staircase. The ground floor comprised the main lounge, dining room, smaller lounge, guest powder room, large kitchen with breakfast area, and a spacious laundry room. On the first floor, there was a small, cozy sitting area at the top of the stairs, a master suite with dressing room and two suites with a bedroom—each with its own separate bathroom. All three bedrooms on that floor had direct access to large balconies overlooking the glorious countryside.

On the top floor, there was a delightful open plan attic with panoramic views of the coast and the hinterland, which, from the smaller windows, seemed to be even more breathtaking than from the first floor. *What a great studio this could be!* Laura thought to herself.

"Oh, I forgot to mention," said the agent, "the house also has a basement. I'll show you that on our way out."

"Obrigada, Sr. Manuel!" Laura thanked the realtor in his native language. "Yes, I would *love* to see it!"

Walking through the kitchen, Manuel grabbed a flashlight he'd hidden at the back of one of the higher shelves—he clicked the button to turn on the light. Laura followed him down the narrow, stone staircase, which led to the basement.

Holding the flashlight high for Laura to look around the sandstone basement, the agent said, "The light bulbs need to be changed. They're all blown."

"Yes, it's very dark," Laura replied, "but I can see just fine, thank you. It seems to be of a reasonable size. It can be used as a wine cellar—which I believe is its original purpose—or I could use it as a storage room."

Back outside, Laura saw there was a swimming pool in the middle of the backyard. Only a few meters away from the rear of the house, it was surrounded by a covered terrace with barbecue area, kitchenette, and a separate bathroom. Further down the backyard, there grew a profusion of fruit trees: oranges, mandarins, lemons, lime, figs, apples, and peaches.

The area surrounding the property included a small pine forest, the unkempt gardens, and a most pleasant surprise for Laura. Delighted, her eyes fixed on the charming old chapel.

"The house was built in 1930 by devout Catholic nobility," Manuel explained as they explored inside the quaint stone chapel with its wonderful sights and smells, the old wooden pews, and stained glass windows—it was all in desperate need of extensive of restoration to bring it back to its former glory. There remained a few artifacts dotted around the chapel, however. In particular, Laura espied a stunning medieval iron chandelier, which hung from the center of the cathedral-style ceiling; Laura knew it would certainly make a statement once brought back to life.

Once they returned to the house—Laura wanted to take a second look inside and make a closer inspection of the fireplace and the burned area—she asked Manuel, "Okay, how much do they want for the place?"

"As it is, the asking price is nine hundred and fifty thousand Euros," he told her.

Laura gasped. "That's far too high! The house needs a heck of a lot of work—and a great deal of money spent on it! My offer is seven hundred thousand Euros, and that's being generous because I can see the house's potential."

"It's been on the market for quite some time, and the owner really wants to sell," the agent told Laura. "I need to contact them—I'll see what I can do for you."

Manuel dropped Laura off at her hotel before driving back to his office to contact the manor house's owners.

"Obrigada, Sr. Manuel," Laura said as she climbed out of his car.

"I'll let you know as soon as hear back from the owners."

"Okay!" She gave him a broad smile. "I'll be waiting!"

The very next day, Manuel called Laura and asked if she could meet him at his office.

"Okay," he began, "the owners are well aware of the condition of the house—but also of its enormous potential. They argued that its position is quite unique, too! All that being said, they are prepared to accept seven hundred and fifty thousand." He paused to gauge Laura's reaction. "This is the very best I could do for you, Miss Laura. They won't be prepared to drop any lower than that."

"Seven-fifty... Hmmm..." repeated Laura. "Can you recommend someone local to help restore the house that is not astronomically expensive? I'm afraid don't know anybody here."

"Yes, of course," Manuel declared. "Antonio is a local builder who's been doing this type of work for many years—especially for foreigners who are buying a lot of property here at the moment. He speaks English very well and has an excellent reputation—and his prices are most reasonable."

Laura listened intently to the realtor. "Okay, then," she said, "we have a deal! I'll accept the offer! And could you please give me Antonio's phone number?"

Having British citizenship, which she acquired following her marriage to Frank, meant Laura was free to buy property and work in Portugal—a member of the European Union. All she needed to do was apply for a Personal Fiscal Number through the local tax office.

Manuel organized all the necessary paperwork and just a few days later, Laura signed the documents at his office. "Congratulations!" the realtor exclaimed as Laura placed her final signature on the dotted line. "You just bought yourself a beautiful house and, may I say, snagged yourself a bargain too! You'll never regret this, Miss Laura—it's one terrific investment!"

"That's just the thing, Sr. Manuel, this is a *home* and not an investment," she answered with a smile. "And a lot of hard work, too!" she added happily. Laura had fallen in love with the old manor house; it was certainly full of potential, but she was also painfully aware of the amount of money she would have to spend to restore it.

That night, before going to bed, Laura called Libby. "Hi, Sis! I've got big news for you!"

"Really?" Libby sounded a tad hesitant. "From the tone of your voice, I'm guessing it's *good* news?"

"You'll *never* guess," Laura said, giggling like a small child.

"You've got my attention now—so do tell!"

"I just bought an awesome old manor house in Sintra!" Laura blurted out.

"*Seriously?!*" Libby exclaimed.

"Oh, yes! I'm *deadly* serious, Sister!" Laura laughed. She was feeling the happiest she had since that fateful day she'd caught Frank and Gina on his desk.

"What about your work?"

"That's on hold for now," Laura explained. "However, I can work from anywhere—I'll be contacting the United Nations Office in Lisbon about that shortly. For now, I've other things on my mind."

"Well, Laura, congratulations!" Libby said. "If that's what you want, then I'm very happy for you. I guess Mark and I will have to return to Portugal for our next holiday!"

"Definitely, Libby!" Laura replied. "I can't wait to have you over! I have a lot of work to do before then, though—I am going to completely renovate the house!"

"I can't wait to see it. Keep me posted, Sis!"

"I will! And... thank you for all your support. I love you!"

"That's what family's for!" Libby said. "I love you, too. Goodnight, Laura."

"Goodnight."

Of course, renovating such a huge house was something completely new to Laura. Feeling both terrified and excited in equal measures, she knew she would require a good team behind her for support on so many levels. Nonetheless, she was absolutely determined to achieve her goal to bring the manor house back to its glamorous grandeur.

Laura loved Portugal so much. It was such an amazing country, and now she had a stunning house in Sintra—that was just the strawberry on the top of the cake!

Never one to be afraid of new experiences and stretching herself to her limits, Laura had proved herself over and over again. She was an achiever, who just loved to be challenged, and this restoration project would not only keep her young and alive, it would distract her mind from her latest disappointments. Laura was a naturally positive person who firmly believed everything in life happened for a reason, and that in time all would fall in the right place. Regardless of all the struggles she'd encountered thus far in life, Laura had always managed to overcome them. And now, she was ready to do it all over again by embracing this new project with all the energy and passion she had in her body. Sometimes it's just the little things in life that count—when they really make you happy.

So this was it!

Laura was ready to change her life by taking on a whole new direction. What she truly desired the most was peace of mind and a happy existence. For now, the manor house in Sintra was the place she was ready to call home.

That night, Laura slept like a baby. In her excited mind, a storm of ideas whirled around and made ready to make her dreams a reality.

Chapter 4

Once she got through the bureaucracy and red tape, Laura met Antonio Domingo, the experienced builder the real estate agent had recommended. Antonio inspected the entire manor house, inside and out, and discussed with Laura her ideas on restoring the amazing period property to its former glory. The two got on incredibly well from the beginning, which was the first step for their great working relationship.

Antonio was a sixty-year-old man with thirty-five years' experience in his field. Tall, robust, with gray hair and a thick mustache, Antonio was a friendly fellow who enjoyed a good reputation among both the locals and expats—the latter of whom, like Laura, had chosen Sintra to be their new home. As such, Antonio was accustomed to dealing with people from all over the world and all walks of life.

Antonio was calm but assertive, and had an astounding attention for detail; he discussed with Laura all of the work that would be necessary restore the manor house and its considerable estate—including the chapel and swimming pool area.

Laura felt at ease with the man. She was more than confident that Antonio's vast experience would be of great benefit to her new house. She knew very well that she needed all of his support and expertise, and she felt in her gut she could trust Antonio completely.

For the landscaping, Antonio recommended a well-known local landscaper, Francisco Xavier. The two men had worked on projects together for many, many years, and always recommended each other.

The next day, Laura met Francisco and Antonio to discuss the more than ambitious landscaping project—Laura's main focus was to be on the area surrounding the delightful chapel; with such beautiful views and endless photographic opportunities, she envisioned it being an ideal venue for local and international guests for romantic weddings. Laura also knew it was a fairytale place from which she could generate a nice, steady income for herself.

Antonio and Francisco took everything in hand and made all the necessary arrangements for the restoration of Laura's property. They made sure to employ only the very best tradesmen in the area, and to make sure the work represented exactly what Laura wanted.

Shortly after the work began, almost a dozen workmen descended upon the manor house. They set to repairing the rotten wood, broken windows, dangerously out of date electrics, and ancient plumbing. Meanwhile, Francisco and his army of gardeners worked diligently on the landscape design. They brought in diggers, tractors, and backhoes to rebuild the garden's retaining walls, lay new grass, and plant new trees along with myriad white flowers. As per Laura's request, the garden was to be all green and white.

With the restoration well underway, Laura soon got to know the name of each and every one of the tradesmen. They, in turn, were all taken by Laura's kindness. She would prepare sandwiches, coffee, and juices for their lunch breaks, and they would all sit together in the pool's barbeque area where Laura had laid out tables and chairs.

Laura was a beautiful, tall young lady with pale blue eyes and long, strawberry blonde hair, which was the perfect complement to her warm skin tone. It was no wonder the workmen were secretly—but *discreetly*—besotted by her. They all maintained a professional respect for Laura, and insisted upon calling her *Miss*!

The youngest man amongst the tradesmen, Carlos, simply couldn't contain his admiration, though. His jaw would drop every time he saw Laura!

"Close your mouth, man!" His colleagues would laugh and mock him. "One of these days you'll catch a fly!"

"Stop dreaming, Carlos, she is not for you!" others would tell him.

Carlos didn't have any aspirations of winning Laura's heart, though. He just couldn't help but be impressed by such a beautiful woman who was so nice and friendly to everyone. She also had such a pretty smile, and when she spoke she brightened *everything*. Sadly, every time Laura addressed him, the shy Carlos would struggle to find something to say. The best he could manage were a mumbled few words in his very poor English.

Of course, Laura needed a car, so she spoiled herself with a white MG sports car with burgundy leather seats—just like one she'd seen as a teenager and had always promised herself she'd own one day. Moving into the house while the restoration work was in progress, Laura occupied the first-floor master bedroom that opened out to a large balcony overlooking the panoramic views of Sintra, the coast, and the hinterland.

It was such a good feeling for Laura to see her home slowly but surely coming back to life. The grounds, too, were also taking shape to provide the ultimate touch of pure, natural beauty she had in her mind.

Meanwhile, Laura met many of the locals and expats as she gradually integrated into Sintra's welcoming society.

As a habitual visitor to the art galleries, Laura got to attend art exhibitions and mingle with expats and locals. She developed a friendship with Chris Smith, the eccentric owner of an art gallery he'd named *ART GLIT*. Chris was a tall, skinny guy with a pony tail and round, John Lennon glasses. He and his wife, Cynthia, an exuberant redhead with truly bohemian style, were both from Ireland. Laura got to know the intellectual, Angela Matias, a thirty-eight-year-old brunette, who was Director of the Sintra Cultural Centre. She also met Steve Bernard, an

English-speaking broadcaster whose breakfast program aired every morning to Sintra's expat residents; he kept them up to date on local issues and national news, cultural commentary, and contemporary music. Steve's wife, Rachel, was an English teacher at the International Language School in Lisbon.

Samantha, the seventeen-year-old daughter of Laura's electrician, Jose Oliveira, came to Laura's aid after school, on weekends, and during school holidays. Samantha helped Laura with chores about the house and assisted with shopping for new décor and furniture. Samantha was also on hand to help Laura with translation on the odd occasion she needed it. English was spoken well by many of the locals, and since Laura was keen to learn the native language, having Samantha around was extremely handy! Samantha, a high school student, received only a small amount of pocket money from her parents—so the money Laura paid her meant a great deal!

Time flew by and the manor house was lovingly restored and freshly painted—just a few finishing touches here and there and it would be completed. Furnishing the magnificent house in the cozy, shabby-chic, vintage style Laura so loved was now well and truly underway, and so Antonio's tradesmen moved on to restore the old chapel.

One day, after bringing back some mugs from the chapel, Laura found Samantha crying in the kitchen—the young girl had just delivered a plate of sandwiches they'd both prepared for the workmen. "Samantha? What's happened?" Laura was concerned.

"Nothing," Samantha replied through her tears. "Nothing has happened!"

"Come here," Laura coaxed. Holding Samantha's hand, she took her to sit in the small seating room adjacent to the kitchen. "Come on, Samantha, please talk to me. What's bothering you?

"I don't want to talk about it," Samantha sobbed, "it's just something silly."

"It doesn't matter if it's silly or not," Laura reassured her. "You're crying for a reason. Please tell me what it is."

"It's George," the girl sniffled.

"George?" Laura was puzzled. "Which George? Is he a boy from your school?"

"No, *George*—the apprentice carpenter at your chapel."

"What has he done to you?"

"Nothing!" Samantha seemed shocked by Laura's suggestion. "He didn't *do* anything. That's the problem; I'm invisible to him!"

"Ah, I see…" Laura replied with a smile. "That's what this is." She felt relieved it was nothing more serious than unrequited teenage love. "Do you like George?"

"Yes… I think I *love* him!" the tearful Samantha replied. "I took the sandwiches over and he never even looked at me… or said thank you. I just don't exist to him!"

Laura took a good, long look at that beautiful, innocent face. Samantha was medium height, slim, with huge, deep, dark brown eyes, hair over her shoulders, and a little fringe that was a tad too short over her forehead. Samantha was a girl who never took advantage of her natural features—much like a rough diamond that had never been shaped. She always dressed in jeans and oversized, striped shirts, and wore her hair tied up in a short ponytail. With that little fringe, from a distance, Samantha could easily pass for a boy. Looking closer at Samantha's face, Laura got the impression the girl had never had her eyebrows done—they were far too thick and almost joined in the middle, which made them appear darker than they actually were.

It didn't surprise Laura at all that the young girl had fallen for the handsome George. He was a twenty-three-year-old gym addict with green eyes, black hair, and the body of a Greek God—the sleeveless t-shirt he always wore showed that off to perfection. Hence, it was no wonder her heart missed a beat every time she saw him.

Laura had an idea to cheer Samantha up. She'd been taken up on her offer to work in the Law Department at the United Nations office in Lisbon. She hadn't wanted a full-time job—it would have been too stressful at that time in her life and she wasn't too keen on traveling. Attending the office a day or two each week, Laura worked mostly from home via email and phone.

"Samantha, I have to go to the office tomorrow—I would love for you to come with me," Laura offered.

"To Lisbon?" Samantha was taken aback. "What am I going to do there while you're at the office?"

"Do you trust me?"

"Yes, of course I do. But I don't understand what it has to do with George." She frowned at Laura. "That's what we *were* talking about, wasn't it?

"You'll understand tomorrow—I promise. I have a surprise in mind for you." Laura gave the girl a warm smile. "Now, go tell your parents you're coming to Lisbon with me. Since it's the school holidays, I don't think they'll mind!

"Okay," Samantha replied. Already she seemed to have brightened up a little. "I'll tell my parents. I'll be delighted to go to Lisbon with you."

"Wonderful," Laura said. "Be here in the morning—no later than eight."

Samantha arrived at the house an hour earlier than requested—she was just *so* excited to go to Lisbon with Laura. For her, it was such a wonderful adventure as it had been a long time since she'd last visited the big city with her parents, and that had been to visit relatives.

After a morning cup of coffee, they left for the capital city in Laura's MG. Less than an hour later, they arrived in Lisbon and Laura parked her car at the United Nations Car Park offices. Before going into the office, she revealed her secret news to an excited Samantha—she had booked an appointment at a nearby hairdresser's for her.

"Louise is my stylist, and she's very good," Laura said. "I think a change of hairstyle would cheer you up—Louise will talk to you about what would best suit your face and bring out your natural beauty. It's a present from me!" She gave Samantha a hug. "I also suggest you have your eyebrows done to bring out your beautiful eyes and brighten up your pretty face. What do you think?"

"Of course!" Samantha replied. "Just look at *you*! You're living proof of Louise's awesome work. Your hair always looks so beautiful—and your eyebrows too! I'd love to have your stylist work on my hair. My mum's the one who usually cuts it."

"Okay then, let's go to talk to Louise." Laura smiled at Samantha's excitement. "I'd booked an appointment for you already—I really didn't think you'd say no."

"It's very kind of you, Miss," Samantha said with a tear glistening in her eye. "Thank you so much."

They walked to the salon, which was less than a block away from the United Nations Office, and on the opposite side of the street.

"Good morning, Louise," Laura greeted the stylist.

"Good morning, Laura." Louise smiled to see her favorite client. "Lovely to see you."

"This is Samantha—the young lady I told you all about."

"Hello, Samantha," Louise held out her hand to shake. "How are you?"

"Very well, thank you, Miss Louise. It's nice to meet you." She shook the stylist's hand and grinned broadly.

"Okay, ladies, I'll leave you in peace," Laura said. "Come meet me at the office when you're finished, Samantha." And with that, Laura rushed off to work.

Louise discussed with Samantha all that needed to be done: her hair styled to suit her face, foils to bring out her hair color, and a treatment and hair massage to bring her dry hair to a silky, smooth texture. She also agreed to shape Samantha's eyebrows into a more modern style, as they had no real shape or form.

"I'm totally in your hands," Samantha said with an excited grin. "Please, do whatever you think is best for me." Just like any girl her age, she was beyond excited at the prospect of a whole new look.

Meanwhile, in the office, Laura, as director of Aid Program, played a big part in Portugal's commitment to take an active role in implementing humanitarian programs to improve the health and wellbeing of the people of East Timor. The overall aim was to work alongside the country's government and support their priority and programs to end poverty. Laura placed particular focus upon improving nutrition and empowering women and girls, through education and employment.

During the regular office meeting, exciting news awaited the executive team. They had all received invitations to attend the Gala Awards promoted by the United Nations Correspondent Association in New York. Laura would be joining the Executive Director, Antonio Serpa, the Deputy Director, Luisa Monteiro, the Director of Program Division, Gil Oliveira, and the Chief and Senior Adviser for Early Education, Vanessa Pinto.

They were all overjoyed. Theirs was an efficient, cohesive team that worked hard and helped each other to deliver the best results. There were stressful times, obviously, but they had all developed such wonderful working relationships with one another. Vanessa Pinto, in particular, had such a great sense of humour; the vivacious, chubby brunette always managed to lighten the mood by cracking corny jokes to make her colleagues laugh. On the other hand, the far more serious and reserved Gil Oliveira usually kept to himself. The team enjoyed some social activities together—they took time out for lunch or dinner together, or would catch up for drinks over the weekends. All of this helped strengthen their relationships.

Leaving the best to last, Laura was honored and humbled to learn she was to the recipient of an award in recognition for all her good work with the organization. When Antonio Serpa handed her the letter and the invitation, Laura was thrilled and quite lost for words.

It was almost lunchtime when Samantha finished up at the salon and came over to meet Laura at the office. The girl looked absolutely amazing!

"Well, well, well! Just look at you!" Laura was delighted with Samantha's new look. "You look totally gorgeous, girl!" Samantha did indeed look stunning and simply radiated a whole new confidence when she smiled.

"I'm so happy!" Samantha said. "I can't believe my eyes—I don't think even my mum will recognize me!"

"Not just your mum," Laura laughed along, "*I* hardly recognized you!"

Louise had done an amazing job to give Samantha a perky, cute look. The uneven, subtly curled tousled effect of her short bob style was decidedly sexy and stylish, and its mixture of honey and coffee color foils made a bold statement in bringing out the hair's natural color. Samantha would have no difficulty standing out in the crowd with such an edgy presence and quirky style!

Samantha's newly tamed, once-bushy eyebrows were now a beautiful enhancement to her big, dark brown eyes, and bright pink lipstick perfectly accentuated her new hairdo to complete her amazing new style. Laura had also organized her makeup—yet another wonderfully unexpected surprise for young Samantha.

"What a day I've had!" Samantha gushed as she hugged Laura. "I've never in my life had a day like this! I feel like Cinderella."

"Let's go," Laura said. "It's time for lunch. The day hasn't finished quite yet; I've got more in store for you, young lady."

"More?" Samantha was puzzled. "You've already done so much for me, Miss. What more could there possibly be? Are you going to find me a prince?" she joked with a gorgeous smile.

"Maybe… who knows?" Laura replied with a wink.

The two went for lunch at an excellent seafood restaurant in the lively, vibrant atmosphere of Baixa, which was in the central, downtown area of the city. They enjoyed Laura's favorite—the traditional *Acorda de Marisco,* which was a typical Portuguese dish of seafood and bread stew.

Following lunch, Laura took Samantha around the very best fashion boutiques in the area. There, Samantha spent ages trying on all manner of dresses, skirts, pants, shirts, and blouses until she ended up with a whole new wardrobe. She then bought sandals, shoes, and boots to complete her beautiful outfits.

It warmed Laura's heart to see Samantha so jubilant. "Let's see if we can find you that prince!" she said.

"Aha! We need *two* princes—one each!" Laughed Samantha. "I really don't know how to thank you, Miss Laura. You've been so lovely and kind—I just hope one day I can repay you for everything you've done for me."

"It's been my pleasure, darling," Laura told her. "You are a treasure of a girl. You don't know it, but you also give me more than you ever can imagine."

"Like what?" Samantha was genuinely puzzled.

"Your delightful company, for one. And all the help you've given me with the house," Laura replied. It truly had been an absolute pleasure to spoil the girl.

Sadly, their day had to come to an end and Laura drove them back home to Sintra. There, the workmen had finished for the day, and Laura invited Samantha to have dinner and sleep over. She had a lot to do the following morning and would need Samantha's help. Samantha was thrilled, of course, as she always enjoyed Laura's company. Different to most girls her age, Samantha was more the quiet kind of girl who preferred to keep to herself, so being with Laura was a great joy.

The next day, this time for different reasons, Laura needed to go to Lisbon again. It was not for business this time—it was time to work on furnishing the house. Laura knew of some wonderful rustic, vintage retail shops in the city, and Samantha was to accompany her on the trip.

Wearing a cute little cream and turquoise dress with a thin black belt around the waist to show off her slender body shape, Samantha looked absolutely gorgeous! She accessorized her outfit with turquoise pendant earrings, and nude and turquoise summer sandals. Laura helped with a final touch of simple makeup—finished off with pink lipstick to accentuate Samantha's full, pouting lips. "Take a look in the mirror," she said to Samantha.

"Woo! I can't believe it's me!" Samantha enthused. "Thank you so much, Miss." She planted a kiss on both of Laura's cheeks.

"Before we leave, we must prepare sandwiches and a jug of orange juice for our boys," Laura said. She often fondly referred to her tradesmen that way.

With the work all but finished, there weren't too many men working anymore. The beautifully manicured front garden was done, and the landscaping surrounding the chapel was still going on but was very close to completion. Those tradesmen who remained were working on the final stages of the chapel's restoration.

Samantha packed the basket onto the cute new vintage bicycle Laura had bought for herself. She always lent it to Samantha to deliver the sandwiches, a huge bottle of orange juice, and fruits from the backyard to the workmen. Samantha rode down to the chapel to place the food and drink on the small table outside. "Good morning!" She popped her head into the chapel to greet the men. "I've left your lunch from Miss on the table."

Someone always turned around to thank Samantha with a broad smile. This time it was Roger, the bear-like carpenter, who stopped short of his casual greeting. He simply didn't recognize the girl standing in the chapel doorway. "Hein! Ahh, thank you... miss...?" He was completely caught by surprise.

"You're most welcome, Roger," Samantha replied.

"How do you know my name?" Roger asked. "Do I know you?"

"It's me, Samantha! Don't you recognize me?"

Overhearing the conversation, and most curious, the other workmen turned their heads around to look at the new girl—all but George.

"Samantha? *Our* Samantha?" exclaimed Rafael, the skinny plasterer.

"Not *your* Samantha, just Samantha," she replied with a cheerful smile and a twinkle in her eye.

George recognized Samantha's voice, of course, but he was immersed in his work and refused to be distracted by the idle conversation. Taking no notice, George kept on working and listening to his music.

Gary, the man closest to George, kicked his leg. *"George, look!"*

"What?" George was annoyed at the interruption. "Can't you see I'm busy?"

"Just *look*, you dumb thing!" Gary whispered.

Convinced it was a prank of some sort, George looked behind. It was as if a lightning bolt had struck him! He froze as his eyes fixed on Samantha. His jaw dropped open, and he was lost for words.

"I'm going to Lisbon with Miss. I'll see you tomorrow," Samantha said without as much as a glance in George's direction—just as Laura had advised.

Gary patted poor George on the head. "You'd better close your mouth before you swallow a fly, George." He laughed and all the other men joined in.

George's hormones kicked in as he looked at Samantha in a whole new way. "What the heck?!" He blurted out the moment she'd left the chapel doorway. "What happened to her?"

Like a butterfly emerging from its chrysalis, Samantha's transformation had seen her blossom into a beautiful young woman. Even her astonished parents were beside themselves when she arrived home later that evening with her new look!

Chapter 5

nd from that day on, Samantha kept delivering the sandwiches and juice. And each day, in George's eyes, she looked even more beautiful and desirable than the day before.

Sticking to Laura's advice, Samantha never once looked George in the eye. He, in turn, watched Samantha like a hawk and craved her attention. He'd smile, say hello, and offer to help Samantha unpack the lunch basket. Samantha thanked him with a coy smile that made his head spin—much as it did with the other workmen who helped her unpack. She continued to pretend to not notice George and treated him no differently than she did the others. The other tradesmen constantly mocked George over him not getting anywhere with winning Samantha's affections.

Laura, meanwhile, was still coaching Samantha. "Let him come to you," she told her, "just take your time and wait. George won't be able to resist much longer without making a pass at you."

"Do you think so?" Samantha was beginning to wonder if George was actually interested in her at all.

"I don't *think*, I'm absolutely positive, my girl! Just you wait and see." Laura and Samantha then took off once again to Lisbon on their quest for the perfect furniture.

A few days after their second trip to Lisbon, the vintage and rustic furniture Laura had bought from the exclusive specialty shops there arrived.

From inside the house, Samantha hit the button to open the new automatic gate. A large truck drove up the driveway and parked as close as possible to the front door of the manor house. Then, two huge, strong deliverymen proceeded to lug the furniture into the house and place it where Laura indicated.

There was a mixture of rustic furniture in subtle pastel colors with a vintage eclectic style, which evoked the romance of Sintra and was the perfect combination for the manor house. To favor the neutral pastels of the distressed, antique woods, Laura chose spots of bright and refreshing color. She added navy blue, lavender, and ivory flowers, sumptuous pillows, and wall art—some of the latter she painted herself. She also incorporated the washed-out pastel of cozy, light cream fabrics. All in all, the shabby chic interior decor brought out the very best in the old manor house.

To complement her eclectically stylish home, Laura adorned the darker spaces with opulent glass vases, antique floral pots, huge stainless steel bowls, and silver ceramic kittens to add a touch of shine and glamour.

To fill an empty or darker corner, Laura added a feminine touch with tablecloths decorated with knots, ruffles, lace, and tassels. She also made good use of the famous Portuguese handmade rugs—*Tapetes de Arraiolos*—in different shapes and sizes.

It had taken almost two full years to get the all done, and Samantha had been more than delighted to help Laura pull everything together. Endlessly fascinated by Laura's amazingly good taste, the girl had never before in her life seen a house as beautiful.

In the living room, Laura took a step back to check everything was in its right place and looking good. She swapped around some pillows and vases before stepping back again to see the result. It was then she realized one of the wooden tables would look much better in a corner of the lunchroom area. And so, with Samantha's help, she attempted to move it. Unfortunately, it proved a little too heavy for them, so Laura asked Samantha to pop over to the chapel and ask one of the workmen to come over and help. "Be sure to ask the question in general," Laura told her. "And definitely *not* directly to George." Laura knew all too well Samantha was always anxious to see the young man. "Wait to see if he offers to come and help."

"Okay, Miss, I'll just do that," Samantha replied with a cheeky smile as she set off for the chapel.

And so, upon entering the chapel in her cute pink top and white shorts, which showed off her long, slender legs wonderfully, Samantha addressed the workmen. "Miss needs to move a table. She asked me to come to see if anyone would help us out. It's far too heavy for us!"

Before any of the workmen had the chance to reply, George jumped at the opportunity. He dropped everything and walked straight over to Samantha. "I'd love to help," he said with a shy smile. With that, George accompanied Samantha out of the chapel and over to the manor house.

Shrugging their shoulders, the other tradesmen looked at each other and laughed. "I thought the boy would never pluck up the courage!" Roger declared loudly.

George counted his blessings as he walked beside the beautiful Samantha. For the two weeks since she'd adopted her new look, he'd been trying to catch her attention. His efforts, sadly, had all been to no avail, as the girl had simply taken no notice of him at all. Like Samantha had experienced before, he'd felt invisible in her eyes.

"I'm very glad to come and help." George was determined to make conversation. "You and Miss Laura have been really busy with the house—thank you for bringing us lunch every day."

"Yes, we've been very busy," Samantha replied. "And there's still a lot more to do. I've been shopping a few times with Miss to Lisbon for furniture, and now she's busy decorating."

"It must be looking beautiful inside."

"It is! Miss has wonderful taste."

"How about you, Samantha?" George enquired. "What else have you been up to in your school holidays?"

"Nothing much," Samantha admitted. "I enjoy being with Miss and helping her with the house. She takes me out for nice lunches—and the other day we went to the beach together. We had a really fun day!"

"You know…" George sounded a tad nervous. "The music festival is starting this weekend. Would you like to come with me? There's an indie rock band—Cosmos—I've always wanted to see live, and they're playing at Pena Park. Perhaps we could go together?"

Thrilled beyond words, her heart exploding with emotion, Samantha just wanted to jump into George's well-toned arms and hug and kiss him. However, she remembered Laura's wise words and managed to contain herself. She kept her cool and calmly responded, "That would be really nice, George. Thank you for inviting me." She was touched to see him blush a little. "I was thinking of asking a friend to go with me—I'd heard about it and really wanted to go."

"Great!" George could barely contain his own excitement.

While walking to the house, the two discussed where in the town center to meet up the following Saturday, and at what time. Finally, George and Samantha were getting together!

Inside the house, Laura wasn't at all surprised to see George accompanying Samantha—it had gone exactly as she'd planned. "Thanks for coming, George," she greeted the handsome young man. "I'd like to move this table from this corner to just below that window. It's solid oak and a bit too heavy for us girls. Would you mind?"

"Of course, Miss," George said with a lopsided grin. With little effort, he grabbed the table and placed it just in the right spot. "Can I help you with anything else while I'm here?"

"No, thank you, George. That's all for now. I really appreciate your help."

"Please, call me anytime you need help, Miss. It would be my pleasure."

"I will, thank you, George."

As soon as George left, Samantha could no longer contain her excitement. "Oh my God, *Miss*! He asked me to go with him to see a live band next weekend!"

"Oh, what a surprise!" Laura rolled her eyes in mock disbelief. "What did I tell you, Samantha? Play it cool and he'd pluck up the courage eventually."

Returning to Sintra every year sometime between May to July, and lasting three consecutive weeks, the unique International Classic Music Festival of Sintra was founded in 1962 by *Marquesa de Cadaval*. It represented an amazing spectrum of modern music styles— in the form of classical music recitals, ballet, and modern dance. For decades, the wonderful festival had brought families and the entire Sintra community together.

A breeze came from afar on that warm June day. It refreshed the streets of the beautiful, fairytale town of Sintra, which, once again, had dressed up for the joyous music festival and feasts. The streets were packed with visitors from all over the world, who happily rubbed shoulders with the easy-going locals to enjoy the fantastic atmosphere. The music was contagious and everywhere—from the huge outdoor concerts to Sintra's many historic monuments.

Wandering along the streets, Laura spotted the familiar faces of fellow expats and the tradesmen who'd worked for her—the latter accompanied by their wives and children. They'd all smile and wave when they saw her. Laura even spotted George and Samantha. They were walking together and holding hands and appeared to be completely smitten by each other. *What a joy to see them so much in love,* Laura thought to herself as happiness filled her heart.

George and Samantha were so in love and had become quite inseparable; they spent all of their free time together. Both were very fond of Laura, and had grown close to her—almost like family. They would often call in on her for a visit, and were always delighted to give a helping hand when needed.

Laura, in return, had developed a deep affection for the two lovebirds. She could see the stars in the young girl eyes when she looked at George, and as for George, he simply adored Samantha. As Laura found out, as she got to know him better, George was a tender, attentive and respectful young man who would do anything to help.

It was lovely for Laura to see them through the windows of her home, and to witness their young love as it flourished. They would sit quietly on her lawns and dream of the promise of a bright future ahead. They planned to spend the rest of their lives together, and to have a family once Samantha finished her education in Early Childhood Education and George completed his apprenticeship—he had plans to start his carpentry own business.

Laura espied a mystic gypsy woman she'd seen a few times before on a corner of the village's main street. Sitting in her old wicker chair with a crystal ball and tarot cards spread over the small table in front of her, the mystic was busy telling a young woman's fortune. The fortuneteller had a most wonderfully bohemian style; she looked most resplendent in a long, flowing, vibrant red, orange and turquoise dress topped off with layers of. She was adorned with many pieces of chunky jewelry, hooped earrings, and layers of long bead necklaces, which she'd mixed with brightly colored scarves. On her slender wrists, she wore large, jangling bracelets of myriad colors, and a silver ring with a large, purple stone stood out from her finger. To complete her look, the gypsy wore a black chiffon headscarf adorned with glittering gold coins wrapped around her long, flowing, raven-black hair.

Laura glanced across at the woman and saw, glued to the wall behind her, a sign with the price she charged for a reading: €20.

And as usual, people were queuing—mostly the younger people of the village and a handful of tourists—all patiently waiting for their turn with the fortuneteller.

The gypsy ignored the prejudice she garnered from the older, deeply religious village women who looked upon her as evil. She even smiled as they blessed themselves and asked for God's protection from evil as they walked briskly by.

As always, the mystic always seemed to sense Laura's presence. She paused her reading for a moment to turn her head and glance at Laura with a small smile.

That's so weird... how on earth does she know I'm here? Laura mused. Remaining on her side of the street, she politely returned the smile.

Laura felt her hands beginning to sweat when the woman glanced at her. It was almost like there was some telepathic connection between Laura and the gypsy woman; it certainly wasn't the first time she'd experienced an inexplicable paranormal phenomenon.

The weird experience brought back to Laura's mind the night her parents were killed. She'd woken up in the middle of the night from a horrendous nightmare, her body soaked with sweat.

In the dream, her parents had been crying and screaming. She'd felt a hand gently touch her forehead, and then the voice of her mother whispering in her ear, "I love you, Laura." She kept the bizarre experience to herself and had never mentioned it to anyone, not even Libby.

Some in the village said the gypsy woman was a genuine medium, and that she had the ability to talk to the dead. Laura had also heard that she would often put curses on people she didn't like.

The next time Laura glanced at the gypsy woman, she beckoned her over. "Come here, young miss!" she called across the street.

Unable to say no, Laura walked over and sat herself down in the newly vacated chair.

The mystic took Laura's hands in hers and, for an instant, closed her eyes. Then she placed her hands over the crystal ball. Taking in a long, deep breath, the gypsy woman began to speak. "Water. I see water. Greenish water... and greenish eyes. Trees... so many trees. I see a man approaching..." She paused, opened her eyes, and added with a smile, "I see a prince, my girl. He will take you away to his castle. I see more water—he is not from here. Go, girl, cross the ocean and follow him. You'll be happy ever after!"

Laura paid her money and thanked the gypsy woman with a beautiful smile. Duly inspired, yet still somewhat skeptical, she walked away from the fortuneteller without really knowing what to make of it all.

Laura saw nothing evil at all about the old gypsy woman with the tender eyes and lovely smile. In fact, she actually felt a kind of warm, relaxed, welcoming aura surrounding the woman. She certainly wasn't the rag-tag, demonized fantasy creature as many painted her to be. To Laura, she was simply a beautiful, exotic lady who was proud of her ethnicity and heritage.

As she continued her meanderings through the cobbled streets, Laura spotted yet another familiar face; the young woman looked uncannily like Claire, her old university roommate. As she got closer, Laura thought to herself, *It can't be! It's not possible!* Intrigued, she walked across the narrow street to the young lady she thought she knew. Taking the risk she may have been wrong, Laura called out, "Claire!"

Hearing her name, the young woman turned around. The look of pure astonishment on her face was a picture to behold! "Laura?! Is that *you*?" She made her way across the street and the two embraced.

"My God! You haven't changed a bit!" Laura exclaimed.

"Neither have you," replied Claire.

"The world is a small place—what are the odds of us meeting in Sintra?" Laura wasn't to know there were more surprises in store.

Suddenly, another familiar face appeared—a young man holding an ice cream in either hand. His eyes met Laura's with disbelief; it was Robert, her ex-boyfriend.

"Robert?" Laura gasped and looked at Claire.

"Laura?!"

"Yes, it's me!" Laura studied the two of them. "Are you two together?" she asked.

"We are," Claire and Robert answered in unison, which Laura thought incredibly cute.

"We're getting married next year," added Claire.

"Well, well, well, what a pleasant surprise. My two favorite people from University are together—that's totally amazing! I'm *so* happy to see you both!" Laura said with a huge smile. "Congratulations to you two lovebirds."

After Laura had finished University, Claire and Robert had stayed back as they both still had another year to go. Robert had missed Laura terribly, and the new girlfriend she had seen him with hadn't lasted long—they'd actually broken up shortly after. Robert knew that Claire and Laura had been roommates and good friends, and at the beginning had taken comfort from Claire's friendship and hearing her news of Laura. Eventually, they'd ended up falling in love and became quite inseparable. Robert and Claire were holidaying in Portugal and had heard about the International Music Festival in Sintra, and that's what had brought them to Laura's new hometown.

"It's Divine intervention!" Laura declared. She smiled at them both. "So, where are you guys staying?"

"Seteais Palace," Robert told her.

"For another two days," Claire added.

"You *must* come over to my house," Laura said. "I live here now."

"Here in Sintra?" Claire was most surprised. "We really do have a lot to talk about, my friend. How come you kept me in the dark about this? You *have* to tell me how you ended up in Sintra!"

"I'll tell you all about it, Claire, and… I have something to show you."

"You do? I can't wait," replied Claire.

Laura and Claire had been such close friends at University, but as often happens in life, they eventually lost touch. Life and circumstances let them drift apart, and they hadn't been in contact for many years. Their lucky encounter in Sintra was a delightful coincidence.

The very next day, Claire and Robert arrived at Laura's house by taxi. They were both absolutely mesmerized by the beauty of the wonderful manor house and its amazing gardens.

After a tour of the house, Laura walked them outside to the pool area. She then escorted them through the proliferation of fruit trees to the enchanting chapel.

Robert and Claire's jaws dropped in unison!

"Wow! What an absolute fairytale!" gasped Claire.

"You said you're getting married next year. So, here we are, this can be your wedding venue; it would be my wedding gift to you."

"Are you serious, Laura?"

"I am deadly serious, Claire," Laura joked.

"Then you *have* to be my maid of honor!" Claire declared with a clap of her hands.

"I'd be delighted."

Back inside the house, they enjoyed a delicious traditional Portuguese seafood rice lunch of *Arroz de Marisco*—Laura had learned the recipe from Samantha's mum, Maria. It was then Laura's turn to tell her old friends the convoluted story of her life so far, which had ended up with her living in Sintra. Of course, Robert and Claire were sorry to hear of Laura's unpleasant divorce, but were delighted to see Laura had that all firmly behind her. She had achieved peace of mind in the little town of Sintra—the place she'd fallen in love with.

A couple of days later, Claire and Robert left for Paris—Claire's hometown—where they lived together. Absolutely over the moon with the prospect of having their wedding in Laura's quaint little chapel in Sintra, they promised to stay in touch.

Chapter 6

Time flew by. Summer came and went. From over the horizon, the winter's cold days drenched the early mornings with a thick, white fog that arrived from the sea. The top of the trees shone each night with frost, and the birds had long since migrated to the warmth of the south.

Laura loved entertaining and showing off her culinary skills. On chilly winter nights, she would invite over her closest local friends Chris, Cynthia, Steve, Rachel, and the fun-loving Vanessa from the office. Other times, she would join them at the local pub for a drink, and then there were the times she'd simply relax in front of a roaring fire with a good book, a warm, comfy blanket over her legs, and a hot chocolate—her favorite drink. How Laura loved to sit back and listen to the crackles and pops of the burning logs in the fireplace. Some nights she would venture up to her cozy studio in the attic. There, she would capture in paint the beauty of the frost she could see from the window.

Three years had passed by since she had last seen Frank. The divorce was finally concluded, via their respective lawyers; Laura didn't want to see, or discuss anything with Frank, and was more than happy to leave it all in her lawyer's hands. An amicable agreement was reached on the division of assets—and the monies were divided fairly.

Thoughts come back to her mind of Frank and the last time she'd set eyes on him. And of how she had run downstairs crying after catching him having sex with the flame-haired Gina on his desk. They'd only spoken once over the phone since that fateful day and Frank had apologized profusely; "I tried to find you," he'd begun. "I wanted to see you and tell you in person just how very sorry I was. And I wanted to tell you it was never about love with Gina… I loved you… and only you."

Laura had interrupted him. "Frank, please, listen. That's all in the past, and what's past is past. I've moved on, and you really don't need to explain anything. It's been a long while, and I don't hold any grudges against you. There's really no point dwelling on it at all—I guess we just weren't meant to be." Laura had cut the conversation short without giving Frank time to reply. "I wish you well. Goodbye, Frank." The line went dead.

Laura knew from her husband's tone that guilt scorched through him, along with the sorrow at having lost her forever. She'd heard him let out a small sigh as she put the phone down as his regret weighed him down.

When Laura moved to Sintra to give herself a clean break, she'd deliberately not let Frank know where to find her.

He'd even called Libby, but she'd refused to tell him where her sister had gone.

It had been a long while and Laura had moved on with her life. She felt at peace; her feelings of betrayal had eased, and she knew there really was no point dwelling on it all.

In truth, the heartbreak caused by Frank's infidelity had been one of the worse things that had ever happened to Laura. Nevertheless, the suffering she'd been through had made her an immensely strong, independent woman. At first, she'd brooded and moped over the failure of her marriage, but eventually she'd grown to see it as a valuable life lesson—one that made her change the course of her life to where she finally felt content. She'd discovered happiness in her inner self, and achieved peace of mind by enjoying the simple, important things in life. Laura had never experienced that in her life before—she'd simply never made the time.

Laura was mature enough to take some of the responsibility for her role in the breakup of her marriage. She and Frank had both been incredibly busy, and she was all too often away working. Towards the end, they had simply taken each other for granted, and unfortunately, Gina had been there for Frank when he'd felt lonely.

Just like the migrating birds, Laura's time came to pack her bags and fly to warmer climes. She'd promised Libby she'd spend a lovely Christmas holiday with her and Mark in Louisiana. And it was there, over the magic night of Christmas Eve, Laura received the best gift she could ever have wished for—she was going to be an auntie! Her dear sister was pregnant with her first baby! Laura enjoyed the night of celebration in the warm company of her family.

Before returning home to Sintra, Laura and Libby visit the cemetery as they used to do as children with Lucy, their grandmother. They lay flowers for their late mother and father. The two lay side by side at the cemetery. This time Laura and Libby also laid flowers to their beloved grandmother who had recently passed away.

When Laura returned home to Sintra in mid-January, winter was still showing its icy ferocity. Surrounded by the warm embrace of her studio, Laura found the panoramic winter views to be the perfect inspiration she needed to paint. It was still too cold to venture outside without risking frozen lips and a bright red nose, so she captured the season's beauty from the comfort of her beautiful home. Laura had truly found heaven in her house. So far away from her busy life, it was the sanctuary she needed to put her mind to rest and recharge her batteries. She had come to think of the manor house as her *retreat*.

Aside from her twice-weekly visits to the UN office in Lisbon, Laura had become quite the homebody. She found contentment and pleasure in the simple things in life—things she'd never had the time to enjoy before: reading, cooking, gardening, and, above all, painting in her haven. There, brushes, a palette knife, sketchbooks, charcoal pencils, rubbers, tubs of acrylic and oil paint in every color, along with canvas and wood panels lay spread over her worktable. Amidst Laura's *organized chaos* there were innumerable easels leaning against the walls—some holding finished paintings, others unfinished—and fresh canvasses scattered across the floor.

Classical music drifted from a vintage radio she'd bought from her favorite antique shop in Sintra, and its relaxing sounds accompanied Laura as she painted. To paint, Laura usually wore her hair up in an untidy bun, which was fastened on top of her head with a wide hairpin. Occasionally, she would catch sight of her reflection in a mirror and realize just how funny she looked with paint stains on her nose and all over her clothes!

Finally, the spring blossoms arrived! The orange, mandarin, lemon, and lime trees bloomed to give a hectic splash of color to the gardens. This came as a welcome contrast to the peaceful green of the fresh leaves and whites of the flowers that gave the garden a stunningly clean, tranquil look. Laura's garden was an invitation for beautiful birds of different kinds: cuckoos, waders, passerines, goldfinch, and myriad others, all of which brought along their own splash of color and vibrant life as they flew from tree to tree to sing their many songs in perfect harmony. Adding an amazing pop of bright colors to the lovingly restored gardens, strikingly patterned butterflies danced their way over the white flowers and verdant shrubs.

All in all, Laura had created a veritable festival of color.

A year had passed, and Claire had been in contact with Laura ever since they'd bumped into one another in Sintra—Claire and Robert had made arrangements for their wedding and had finally chosen the date. Claire discussed the wedding plans with Laura, which included the decorations, menu, flower arrangements, photography, and the live entertainment. Laura provided Claire with the contacts she needed and was happy to be a helping hand in coordinating everything in Sintra; after all, she was the maid of honor and felt a warm sense of duty. She was truly excited for Claire and Robert, and was determined they should have a most memorable wedding day.

Claire and Robert arrived a week early for the final touches and rehearsal at the chapel. Laura had organized an English-speaking Roman Catholic priest officiate their union.

Laura's garden was in full splendor; Spring was simply the perfect time to celebrate Claire and Robert's union.

"We're so happy to be back, Laura," Claire gushed. "Thank you *so* much for all your help. And thank you, too, for letting us stay at your beautiful house, *and* for such a wonderful venue for our wedding ceremony." An emotional Claire tenderly embraced Laura, her eyes filled with tears of joy.

"I'm as excited as you—believe me. Laura couldn't help but shed a tear or two herself. "I'm so thrilled you two accepted my offer, and I'm delighted to be your maid of honor!"

Laura showed Claire and Robert to the guest room. "Come on, make yourselves comfortable. I have much to do downstairs, so take your time." She left them alone to unpack.

After a while, they joined her downstairs where they savored a coffee together, along with a little chat about their trip. "It's such as short trip—only two and a half hours from Paris to Lisbon," Claire told her. "So there's absolutely no excuse for us not to visit each other more often. We will never lose contact again."

"No we won't. I promise you that," Laura replied. "Now, I have to show you something. You haven't seen my dress yet…"

"Oh my God, Laura. Yes, I've been dying to see it! I'll show you mine, too."

"Okay girls," Robert said with a smile. "I think it's time for me to leave you two alone. I'm going to wander down to the village center and do some shopping; I'm cooking dinner tonight."

"Claire didn't tell me you could cook," Laura said. "That would be wonderful."

"Oh yes, Laura, Robert is a terrific cook. He always does the cooking at home—I really am quite awful at it, so it's a blessing." Claire sounded cheerful.

"Okay then. I'll see you both later. I'll do my best to impress you girls with dinner."

"Here, take my car keys." Laura tossed the keys to Robert. "Everything is nearby here, so you'll easily find your way around."

"Thank you, Laura. Yep, I'll find my way—don't you worry about that." Robert left Laura and his bride-to-be in peace and the two showed each other their dresses, and tried them on just like a pair of giddy teenage girls.

They were both over the moon, of course, to be able to catch up on the gossip, just as they had in the old good times they'd shared at university. The main theme of the conversation was, naturally, the wedding; the fifty or so guests, mostly family and close friends from Paris and London, were delighted the wedding was to be in Sintra. It made for a good excuse to extend their time and enjoy a little holiday in Portugal, which some had never visited before. They had all booked into the Sintra's hotels, and had provided quite a boon for the local economy.

Later that afternoon, Robert prepared a splendid roast pork dinner, and the three enjoyed a pleasant night talking about their lives, their work, and the blessed coincidence that had brought them together. "Of all odds, who could have ever guessed we'd be here right now?" declared Laura.

One week after their arrival, Robert and Claire tied the knot. Claire was quite the vision when she stepped out in a gorgeous white organza wedding dress; it had sheer paneling at the top of the boat neckline and little pleated caped sleeves. Robert looked exceptionally smart in his classic black tuxedo. Laura, the proud maid of honor, looked elegant in her stunning, pale pink, silk sheath dress with draped sleeves.

It was just the perfect day for Laura's old friends to begin the new chapter of their life together; a day they would forever remember, it was intimate, moving, and beautifully emotional. The idyllic venue couldn't have been more romantic than on that beautiful spring day kissed by a gentle breeze.

The day after the wedding, Claire and Robert departed for their honeymoon in Cuba. "We feel so blessed, Laura," Claire was immensely grateful to her friend. "Thank you for helping us create a once in a lifetime wedding, and for making our day so wonderful."

"It was my pleasure. Thank you for giving me the opportunity to share your special day with you; it made me really so happy." Laura hugged both of her friends and bid then *bon voyage*.

After they left, Laura resumed her usual daily life.

One stunning spring morning, the cloudless sky was blue and the heavens bright and clear. Laura packed up her basket with brushes, paints, canvas, and her easel to ride off on her vintage bicycle to a hidden paradise.

Away from tourists and crowds, back down the hill towards Sintra, Laura set to painting the scenic views of the Valley of the Lakes. It was her favorite spot in the world, which nestled deep in the heart of the Sintra National Park. The beautiful valley featured a series of five man-made lakes in the grounds of the *Palacio da Pena*. It was a truly peaceful area surrounded by flush forests, plants, and flower-covered walls.

And it was there that Laura would meet her Prince Charming.

Marcelo Dubois was a French winemaker from the region of Provence. There, he owned a Chateau and one of the oldest vineyards in France. It had been handed down from generation to generation, and Marcelo had inherited the estate from his father who had passed away two years previously. Marcelo was staying in the Sintra holiday home of a Portuguese friend from Oporto—Diogo Mesquita. Diogo was the owner of the famous, world-renowned Porto Wine from the Douro region, which was one of the most spectacular places in Portugal. Marcelo and Diogo had met through the wine business and had become very good friends.

Marcelo was a great lover of horse riding. During his excursions through the Sintra forests, he was constantly looking for the most picturesque views. Often, he would change his course through the forests in the search of something new.

From away in the distance, he saw the vague outline of a young woman in a small clearing near the lake. He immediately decided to investigate. Curious, he slowed down his horse as he neared the clearing; Marcelo was mindful to not disturb or scare the young woman he *thought* he'd seen. It was like he was seeing a mirage—or perhaps a Renoir painting that fair took the breath away.

As Marcelo drew closer, the hazy image of the young woman by the lake became clearer. It was then he could see she was painting the stunning view of the lake itself. She wore a beige, straw hat, an oversized red and white checked blouse, and blue jeans rolled up to her knees to provide a tantalizing glimpse of her toned, slender legs.

Leaning against a nearby rock was a vintage-style bicycle with wire basket at the front, which was filled with canvas, paper, and brushes.

Marcelo thought the vision was impossibly beautiful and too good to be true. In fact, he had to pinch himself to make sure he wasn't dreaming.

Dismounting his horse, holding the reins in his hand, Marcelo slowly approached the young woman from behind. He made sure to make just enough noise to attract her attention and make his presence noticeable; he much preferred to alert the young woman instead of catching her by surprise and giving her a fright.

Realizing someone was behind her, Laura turned around to see the tall, handsome young man. As she did so, the warm sun illuminated her beautiful face.

Once Marcelo knew the young woman was aware of his presence, he walked closer.

It was a truly magical moment!

Their eyes met. For an instant, they didn't utter a single word. Frozen in silence, they were entirely dazed by one another.

Completely paralyzed by the moment, a sweet tingle of electricity coursed through Laura. When the young man smiled at her, she noticed the cute dimple on his left cheek. Finally snapping out of the intense moment, Laura came to her senses and broke the silence. "Hi, there!" she said.

"Hi," replied Marcelo. "I'm so sorry to interrupt you. It's really my horse's fault—he brought me over." Marcelo joked with a beaming smile.

"So… your *horse* got you lost in the forest?" Laura returned the smile.

"Actually, I'm not sure if he lost me or if he found my way," the gallant Frenchman replied.

"I'm Laura, it's nice to meet you."

"I'm Marcelo." He glanced at Laura's painting. "That's really beautiful," he told her. "Do you sell your paintings?"

"No," Laura replied. "Never. I just love painting."

"You're very talented." Marcelo's smile made Laura melt. "You really should try to sell it."

"Hmmm…" Laura mused. She had little intention of following the stranger's advice, but it was flattering to hear nonetheless. "Maybe one day." She glanced at her watch. "I'm sorry, but it's getting late," she flustered. "I was about to pack up for the day. I don't mean to be rude… but I honestly do have a meeting this afternoon."

"Oh, so soon?" Marcelo appeared genuinely disappointed.

Laura nodded. "That's why I came here earlier today," she said as she packed up her basket.

"I'd love to see the finished result." Marcelo pointed at the painting. "Where may I see it?"

"Well, I'll be here tomorrow if your horse happens to be heading this way." Laura smiled at the young man. "I aim to finish the painting then." She made ready to cycle away.

"If you don't mind my being here while you work, I'll be here tomorrow at the same time. It's been wonderful to meet you, Laura." And with that, the dashing young Frenchman mounted his horse and disappeared back into the forest.

Laura couldn't sleep at all that night. She tossed and turned from one side to the other in bed in her desperation to find a comfortable position to sleep. But it was all in vain. Marcelo simply wouldn't leave her mind. He was just so handsome, and those kind, expressive eyes made him totally irresistible. In their all too brief encounter, Laura had found him charming and witty, and he'd swept her off her feet in a way she'd never experienced before. *I bet he has a million girls falling for him*, Laura thought to herself, and she was surprised to discover the thought made her a little uneasy. Finally, Laura managed to fall into a light, fitful sleep.

Before the sun rose, Laura was wide-awake. She'd hardly slept at all, what with Marcelo's strong arms holding her tight in her dreams. Weary, Laura showered and dressed in her beige overalls.

Shortly after having a strong coffee at her kitchen's breakfast counter, Laura grabbed her bicycle and was on her way. She took a short cut to the lake through the forest she'd gotten to know so well. Preferring solitude when painting, Laura wanted to paint as much as possible to allow plenty of time to talk to Marcelo when—*if*—he arrived.

Time went by as Laura painted. Nervously, she'd check her watch, and occasionally she would look anxiously into the forest to try to spot Marcelo and his magnificent horse. *He's not coming,* she thought to herself, *I was silly to think he would! What was I thinking?*

Feeling a little foolish, a disappointed Laura made ready to call it a day. She was just about to begin packing up when she heard a noise behind her.

Startled, her heart racing, Laura spun around. And, yes, there was Marcelo.

"I'm *so* glad you're still here," Marcelo exclaimed. "I played golf with my friend, Diogo, early this morning, and it took much longer than usual—I had to cut our game short to come here." He climbed down from his horse. From behind his back, he produced a small bunch of wildflowers he'd picked for Laura on his way through the forest. "For you." He gave her a soft smile.

"Oh, thank you." Laura was quite taken aback. It had been such a long time since someone had given her flowers. "That's so very sweet of you—they're beautiful!"

"I can't take all the credit, the forest gave them to me," Marcelo replied with a cheeky wink. He studied Laura's painting on its easel and saw it was almost finished. "Wow, it's beautiful," he gasped. "I really like it, Laura."

"Why, thank you, sir." Laura pretended to be coy.

"Would you allow me to take a picture of you painting at your easel? Just as you were when I saw you for the very first time—with your bicycle leaning against that rock." He smiled at Laura. "And... what can I do to persuade you to sell the painting to me?"

Laura took a step back to look at the Frenchman. "Hmmm..."

"Hmmm what, Laura?" Marcelo looked puzzled.

"Okay," Laura announced. "I have a deal for you."

Marcelo's eyes brightened. "Excellent... what's the deal?"

"I like the view behind you," Laura told him. "It doesn't include the lake, but it is a beautiful view of the forest. I want to take a picture of you right there—holding your horse's reins with one hand and the flowers in the other." She gave him a stunning smile. "And that will be my next painting. I'll give you this one if I can keep the one with you on it. What do you think, Marcelo?"

A broad, toothy smile brightened Marcelo's handsome features. With a twinkle in his eye, he said, "What a great idea, Laura. I will have you and you will have me." He giggled quite suggestively.

"We'll have each other's *pictures…*" Laura corrected him with a cute smile playing upon her lips.

"However you'd like to put it, Laura." Marcelo flirted right back. "We have a deal!"

They laughed together as if they'd known one another for a lifetime rather than just a couple of fleeting moments. Laura had never felt so alive than in the wonderful Marcelo's presence.

Marcelo pulled out his cell phone and opened up the camera app. "If you'd turn to your easel and look as if you're painting, I'll take your picture right now."

Laura was only too happy to oblige—there was just something about the dashing young Frenchman that had her feeling like a giddy, love-struck schoolgirl. Turning to her easel, she resumed adding the finishing touches to the deep blue-green of the lake.

Marcelo snapped the picture. "Beautiful!" he declared.

"It's my turn now," Laura said as she pulled out her cell phone from her pocket. "Take the reins in this hand and…" She handed the flowers back to him. "Hold these." Stepping back, Laura took a second or two to frame the photograph before hitting the button. "Perfect!" she declared.

"What's perfect? Me?" joked Marcelo.

"No… the picture framing is perfect." Laura chose to ignore the man's brazen attempt at garnering a compliment.

She and Marcelo then exchanged numbers so they could send the photographs to one another's cell phones. "I'm finished here for now," Laura said. "I can use the photo to add myself and the bicycle in my studio at home.

"How about the one with me and my horse?"

"Well… I'll come back tomorrow to paint your background," Laura told the Frenchman. "I'll add you both in later. It would be too uncomfortable for you to stand still for so long."

"Okay." Marcelo gave her a grateful smile. "May I come again tomorrow? I promise to keep quiet and let you concentrate. I just love to watch you paint." It was clear he understood Laura preferred solitude in which to paint.

"If you wish." Laura hid the fact that she was delighted. "It may be boring for you, though."

"Not at all. Trust me, I could *never* find you boring. I'll be here, Laura… and on time!"

Laura finished packing up her basket and her sweet posy of flowers. Before riding off into the forest, she shouted after Marcelo, "Thank you for my beautiful flowers!"

"I'm glad you like them!" Marcelo called back over his shoulder. "I'll see you tomorrow, Laura!" He waved a hand over his head. And with that, he disappeared into the forest.

With a sweet smile playing on her lips, Laura unpacked her white basket at home. She lovingly placed the flowers Marcelo had given her in a gorgeous hand-painted glass jar, which she positioned over her worktable in the studio.

Then, sitting down at her computer, Laura uploaded and enlarged the photographs she'd taken of Marcelo by the lake before printing them out. As happy as never before, she then added herself to the painting she'd almost completed. Right there, she had the painting she'd promised to Marcelo to hang in his home!

It looked absolutely amazing, of course. Having put her heart and soul into the painting, Laura was absolutely thrilled with the final result. Just a few more touch-ups here and there, and it would look like a masterpiece.

Gee, I think I'm falling for him already! Laura thought to herself as she busied away with her delicate brushes. *How is that even possible after only meeting twice?* She couldn't help but keep glancing across at the photograph of Marcelo on the corner of her other easel.

It was dark when Laura finally finished the painting. Having totally forgotten to eat dinner, she helped herself to some of the leftover chicken she found in the fridge. Warming up the succulent white meat in the microwave, Laura ate her little dinner all alone at the small kitchen table.

After a refreshing shower, Laura brushed the tangles from her hair and retired straight to bed—she was really quite exhausted. Suddenly, her cell phone rang. Startled, Laura looked to see who it was before answering. It was Marcelo! Her heart raced as she picked up the phone. "Hello?" she said.

"Laura, it's me," Marcelo's voice greeted her. "I just called to say goodnight. And to thank you for today."

"Thank you, Marcelo, that's very thoughtful of you. Thank you for your company, too. Goodnight!"

"Sweet dreams, Laura. See you tomorrow."

Laura couldn't contain her happiness. She fell asleep dreaming about Marcelo—his kind eyes, wonderful smile, great sense of humor, and that sexy accent! For so long, Laura had secretly wished for the day she'd find *the one* for her to love. Could *the one* possibly be Marcelo? Of course, it was far too soon to know for certain if the handsome Frenchman was the one for her; all Laura knew was she had no other craving but to see him again.

That night, Laura slept like a log.

When Marcelo arrived at the lake the following day, Laura was well and truly absorbed in her painting. As she was facing toward the forest this time, she saw him approaching on his horse. She gave Marcelo a broad, happy smile and waved at him. Then, without moving from her easel, Laura continued painting.

Marcelo blew Laura a playful kiss. He carefully maneuvered his horse behind Laura to ensure he gave her the solitude she needed to concentrate. After all, he *had* promised to be quiet and not to disturb her.

Quietly, Marcelo dismounted and opened out a thick woolen blanket on the grass. Relaxed, he sat there and watched as she painted. He was forced to admit to himself that he'd admired, adored, and loved her since that first day they'd met—her sweet, blue eyes lit up his very heart! Since that day, he'd carried her smile into his dreams and thoughts each night. *This is love at first sight, my friend!* he thought to himself, and the thought scared him just a little—he'd never felt that way before.

Close by sat the small picnic basket Marcelo had brought along. It was filled with sandwiches and a bottle of white wine—Monsaraz from Alentejo, the famous region of south central and southern Portugal; it had been Diogo's suggestion—all ready for Laura to take a break from her paints. And, of course, there was a cute posy of wildflowers Marcelo picked on his way through the forest.

After what seemed an eternity, Laura paused her work.

Turning her head to look at her new friend, Laura's heart skipped. Marcelo appeared to be most comfortable on the blanket with the little bunch of flowers clutched in his hand as he waited patiently for her. The shimmering lake was behind him, which enhanced his eyes and charming smile. *How perfectly adorable,* Laura thought to herself.

Laura's stunning beauty reflected upon Marcelo's greenish eyes. *This girl has put a spell on me,* he thought as she made her way over to him. As Laura sat down beside him, Marcelo opened the basket. He took out two glasses, two small plates, the sandwiches, and the bottle of wine. He arranged them all neatly on the blanket.

"Hmm… we have quite a feast here." Laura smiled.

"For you, Mademoiselle." Marcelo handed over the flowers

"You're spoiling me! Thank you."

And for the first time, over a glass of wine, they talked about themselves, their work, their past, and their goals. There was a definite trust building between them, as they openly confided their deepest secrets to one another. It was as if Laura and Marcelo had known each other *forever,* and the beautiful, silent lake was their only witness.

It began to get rather late. As the darkness of dusk was setting in, Laura took the plunge and invited Marcelo over for dinner at her house. "I've got something to show you," she teased.

"I can't wait! I'll ask Diogo to give me a lift to your house…"

"and I'll take you back," Laura completed his sentence.

Remembering something, Laura suddenly leaped to her feet. "Oops! I forgot to close the lids on my tint tubes!" she exclaimed. "I'd best do that before they dry up. It'll only take me a second."

After closing the lids, Laura carefully put them away in her basket. She also added her brushes and the canvas she'd been working on. As had happened countless times before, she accidentally colored her nose and forehead with smudges of paint without realizing. When she sat back down next to Marcelo, he took one look at her and laughed. "You look so cute like that!"

"What!? Why are you laughing at me?" Laura suddenly felt self-conscious.

"Come here." Marcelo gently pulled Laura closer. He plucked a paper napkin from the picnic basket and proceeded to clean her face.

"Ah, that! Yes, of course," Laura said with a giggle—there had been so many times in the past she'd not noticed 'til much later she was smeared with oil paints.

Gently, Marcelo tried to wipe away the paint from her nose and forehead. Unfortunately, he only succeeded in making it worse. Laughing out loud, he declared, "Terrible! I made it *so* much worse! But... you do look *really* funny!" He laughed at Laura's look of indignation. "I think we need water to wash your face." So saying, and totally unexpected, Marcelo stood up and began to undress. Casting aside his shoes and clothes, he proceeded to jump into the cool water of the lake clad only in his boxer shorts. "Come on, Laura, jump in! Ahh… the water is beautiful!" He then slipped off his boxer shorts, threw them to the shore, and swam away from her.

"What are you doing?!" Laura was a little shocked "You're *so* silly, Marcelo!" she shouted after him.

Nevertheless, Laura began to undress. She kicked off her shoes and tossed her overalls and shirt on the grass next to Marcelo's discarded clothes. Giggling, wearing just her bra and panties, she joined him in the water. As Laura submerged, she decided to copy Marcelo's example and strip off her undergarments, which she threw to the shore.

Like two giddy little kids, Marcelo and Laura laughed together, swam, and splashed water at one another. Marcelo checked to see if there was still any paint on Laura's face. Jokingly, he rubbed her nose.

"What?! There's *still* paint in my nose?" Laura pretended to be horrified at the very notion. Facing one another in the water, they looked deep into each other's eyes as Marcelo pulled Laura slowly towards him. The rays of the sun shining upon the water enhanced the color of Laura's eyes, and her natural beauty drove Marcelo's passion. Their naked bodies pressed tightly together as their lips locked in a passionate kiss, and their hearts beat as one as they were overcome with an all-encompassing, fiery desire to experience one another. Embracing in the cool water, Laura's nipples pressed hard against Marcelo's broad chest as he lifted her legs around his waist for her to cross behind his back…

Suddenly, Laura glanced over Marcelo's shoulder. Peering out at the forest, she noticed a distant movement. "Look!" she whispered in his ear.

"What is it?"

She pointed out into the distance. "Rangers!"

With great reluctance, they let go of one another and dived beneath the water. A moment later, like two little turtles, they popped up their heads to scan the area before swimming quickly back to shore. There, they hid behind the rock where Laura's bicycle leaned to watch the rangers ride by. Feeling relatively safe from discovery, they ran over to dry their wet bodies with the blanket before quickly dressing. They'd narrowly escaped being caught skinny-dipping by the rangers and had avoided that embarrassment. The very thought had Marcelo and Laura laughing together like two naughty children.

They kissed a fond goodbye shortly afterward and rode away in opposite directions. "I'll see you later!" Laura shouted at Marcelo's retreating shape as she waved him goodbye.

"I'll be there." He replied and blew her a kiss.

It was 7:30 in the evening when the bell rang at the manor house.

It was Marcelo. Laura opened the gate from inside the house and told him to drive up to the front door. Diogo dropped him off at the door and got out of the car to greet Laura. "Hi, Laura, I'm Diogo. It's a pleasure to meet you. I've heard a lot about you from Marcelo—I hope one day I can see your paintings."

"It's nice to meet you, too, Diogo. Yes, of course, you can see them—someday very soon."

"Excellent! Well, I'll see you both later." Diogo was already climbing behind the wheel of his Maserati and making ready to leave—as much as he wanted to see her paintings, he knew his friend wanted the beautiful Laura all to himself. And, without further ado, he drove off into the fading light.

Laura looked absolutely stunning. She wore a small, black dress, which was complemented by black, high-heeled, strappy sandals. A dab of scarlet lipstick enhanced her plump lips and lit up her beautiful face. Of course, Marcelo had yet to see Laura all dressed up and looking so amazing, classic, and elegant. Thus far he had only seen the girl by the lake dressed in overalls, oversized shirts, and a floppy old hat!

"You look absolutely amazing," Marcelo said. "Here, for you..." He produced a bunch of dark red roses he'd been hiding behind his back. In his other hand, he clutched a bottle of red wine from one of his own vineyards.

"Oh," Laura gasped. "They're so beautiful, Marcelo—thank you. I simply *adore* red roses. She gave him a big smile. "And you look pretty good, too."

Marcelo did look incredibly stylish—and quite irresistible—in black pants, black shoes, and a white, long-sleeved shirt with the top two buttons opened.

Laura invited Marcelo in. Once inside the house, he couldn't help but be impressed by its generous size. "You have a charming house, Laura. I love how you've decorated it—you have exquisite taste. It feels so warm and cozy! I love it!"

"I'll show you the backyard and the gardens another time," Laura told him. "It's getting dark, and I've got food in the oven."

After checking on the food, Laura escorted Marcelo to her studio in the attic to show him the painting that was all ready for him to take home. *"Tada!"* she exclaimed. "Your painting is finished!"

"That's amazing! Thank you *so* much, Laura," Marcelo gushed. "I totally love it! I have a very special place for it at home. Now, how about the other painting... the one with me in it?"

"There." Laura pointed to the other easel. It had a cover draped over it and Marcelo's picture clipped on the corner.

"I'd love to see that one too..."

"You can see it when it's ready, and not before!" Laura chastised Marcelo's impatience.

Finally, dinner was ready. Before bringing out the food, Laura seated her guest at the table. She'd arranged the roses in her favorite crystal vase and placed it in the center of the table. She lit the candles as Marcelo opened the bottle of wine he'd brought with him. Pouring the blood-red wine into two crystal glasses, he proposed a toast. "Cheers, Laura... to us... and to the lake that brought us together!"

Laura lifted her glass and clinked it against his. "To us and our lake," she said. Taking a sip of the delicious wine, Laura served dinner. *"Bon appetite,"* she announced with a satisfied smile.

"This looks beautiful, Laura." Marcelo eyed the mouthwatering array of food she'd prepared for him. "I had no idea you'd be such a good chef!"

"Thank you, but I'm no chef!" Laura laughed. "But I do love cooking. I've done my very best to learn some Portuguese traditional dishes. This is a traditional *carne de porco à alentejana*—pork meat with clams—it's a recipe from Alentejo in Southern Portugal."

"Well, it looks delicious and smells even better," replied Marcelo.

Laura had set the dinner out on a small table on the large balcony off the dining room. A gentle breeze fluttered the delicately woven tablecloth, and the dark sky teamed with a blanket of twinkling stars, which were only broken by the magical glow of the hauntingly full moon. It was simply divine!

Dinner was filled with pleasant conversation, laughs, and lovely moments. As dinner finished and the moon began to rise, Laura lit more candles, and with Marcelo's help, she cleared the table.

The ambience on the veranda couldn't have been more auspicious. Relaxed, with soft music in the background to set the romantic tone, Laura and Marcelo chatted and laughed together without a care in the world. There were gentle touches of hands and arms, and Marcelo stroked Laura's hair as she rested her head upon his shoulder. Sweet glances increased their closeness and created a warm physical and emotional connection.

"This is just a perfect night Laura." Marcelo looked deep into her eyes to ignite the spark that attracted them to each other. "I wish I could read your dreams and make them come true, my sweet love." Moving closer, Laura held his hand, looked into his eyes, and said, "I have something to confess..." she whispered in his ear, "being here with you is a dream come true, my love."

They stood there together on the veranda beneath the stars to admire the silver moon. Laura felt the warmth of Marcelo's breath caressing her face as, tenderly, he pulled her closer. The soft light of the moon enhanced the intensity between them as they embraced and abandoned themselves to a hot, passionate kiss.

"I'm crazy about you," Marcelo broke the kiss to whisper in Laura's ear.

"You're always on my mind, too," she replied.

Lifting Laura into his arms, Marcelo carried her to the bedroom. There, in a passionate frenzy, they undressed each other on the bed. Then they made the most sensual love... over and over again. It was the perfect ending to such a magical, romantic night as, exhausted, they fell into a deep sleep in each other's arms.

The next morning, Marcelo awoke to the sound of voices coming from outside. He gently woke Laura with tender kisses. "Good morning, my love," he whispered in her ear. "I heard voices—are you expecting someone?"

Stretching and still sleepy, Laura replied, "No, my darling. It's just the workmen who are working on the renovations. I invited them and their families to come over today—and next Sunday morning—to pick fruit from the trees. There's far more than I could ever need, so I figured it better to give it away than to waste good fruit."

Laura grabbed Marcelo's button-down shirt from the floor, put it on, and jumped off the bed. "Come here, come with me." She took hold of his hand.

"You look *so* cute wearing my shirt," Marcelo said with a crinkled smile. He took a moment to take in Laura's natural, alluring beauty; he was amazed at how her messy hair made her even *more* sensual and desirable. Then, following her lead, Marcelo jumped out of bed as she opened the large door to the balcony and stepped out in his Bonds boxer shorts.

"Look." Laura pointed to the fruit trees that adorned the backyard. There, beneath the trees, a multitude of men, women, and children were picking oranges, mandarins, limes, and lemons; they placed the plethora of fruit into the wide wicker baskets they'd spread across the grass.

"Some of the wives bring me their homemade jam, and others bring me cakes—they're such beautiful and generous people," Laura told Marcelo. "They're always ready to open their doors to you. If you arrive at a mealtime, they just add another plate to the table—it's just in their kind, loving nature."

"And how do they get in to your garden?" Marcelo was intrigued. "I didn't hear the bell ring, and don't you have to open the gate?"

"No," Laura told him, "Samantha has a spare key for the side gate near the chapel!"

"A chapel?!" Marcelo's eyes lit up. "You have a *chapel*?"

"Yes, I do!" Laura smiled at him. "I'll show you it very, very soon—I promise." She lustfully eyed Marcelo's solid, muscular body as his eyes stirred the passion within her. Unable to resist, she pushed him back onto the bed and jumped on top of him. Kissing and exploring, they made passionate love once more.

Later, after taking a shower together, they enjoyed a light breakfast of orange juice and a ham and cheese croissant, which was followed by a morning coffee on the small kitchen table. "It's time to show you the outside," Laura suddenly announced. "Come on, let's go!"

Laura was wearing jeans and a crisp, white t-shirt, while Marcelo wore the clothes from the night before with the sleeves of his shirt folded up to provide a more casual look. He followed Laura outside to meet the people picking fruit. Laura introduced Marcelo to each one of them in turn, and they all seemed very happy to see Miss with such a handsome young man.

Then, Samantha and George came running over. They were curious to meet the new man in Miss's life. "Good morning, Miss," they said in unison.

"Oh, good morning, George… good morning, Samantha." Laura was delighted to see them. "Where's your mum?"

"She went to mass. She said she might come over later," Samantha explained.

"This is Marcelo," Laura made the introduction. "I wanted to introduce him to your mum—he loved *carne de porco à alentejana* she taught me how to make."

After all the greetings were done, Laura took Marcelo to see the chapel.

"Wow! This is unbelievable," Marcelo gasped as he looked around the well-kept gardens and spectacular views.

He then went inside the gorgeous little chapel. Laura explained to him that she rented it out for wedding ceremonies, which generated a nice, steady income for her.

"You must be fully booked," Marcelo was clearly impressed. "This is absolutely beautiful."

"It's fully booked to the end of the year," Laura told him. "Mostly it's weddings, but there are a few christenings. I don't actually organize anything—I only rent out the venue. The brides and their families do everything else themselves. It's a terrific business, and so easy to run. It actually gives me a good income, too; it covers my expenses with garden maintenance, running the house, and paying some of the bills." She showed Marcelo a box stuffed with business cards from the very best professionals in the area: florists, interior decorators, chauffeur services, caterers, photographers, priests, and wedding celebrants. "I'm always happy to recommend good people, of course."

"Well done, Laura… and congratulations," Marcelo said. He gently pulled Laura to him and tenderly kissed her. "I hate leaving you behind Laura. I wish I could stay longer but it would be a mess to cancel all my commitments. Dammit, responsibility calls."

That evening, Marcelo was leaving for France.

They had discussed it before their wonderful evening together, and had agreed that theirs was too short a time together. They knew they'd miss each other like crazy, so

Laura had invited Marcelo to join her at the Award ceremony in New York.

"I would love to." Marcelo couldn't have been happier. "It would be an honor to go with you, my love." He gave her a big smile. They had agreed Laura would meet him in Marseille and they'd spend some time together before flying on to New York.

"Laura, please come with me," Marcelo implored; it was still painful for him to leave without her. "I really don't think I can live without you—it hurts my heart to think of leaving without you."

"I would love to… but I can't right now, my darling. I know exactly how you feel, but my agenda is fully booked, too. Time will fly and before we know it we'll be together again," she reassured. "It's only two weeks before I meet you in Marseille; it'll be your turn to show me around your house!" She laughed. "I'm so happy you're coming with me to the gala ceremony. That tops everything, my prince charming!"

"Of course. I'm looking forward to witnessing the *coronation* of my princess." Marcelo was back to his playful self. "And I can't wait to show you my home… and Provence."

"I've heard such wonderful things about Provence." Laura could barely contain her excitement. "I've only ever been to Paris, and I just *love* Paris…"

"I know you're going to fall in love with Provence," Marcelo told her. "It is also very beautiful."

"*You* will be there, Marcelo, and that's what will make it beautiful."

Laura drove Marcelo back to Diogo's holiday home, which was an impressively renovated palace. Not having enough time to go inside, Laura left Marcelo at the door—he needed to pack his bags and catch his flight in Lisbon. They embraced and stole a kiss goodbye for one last time.

She had offered to take him to the airport, of course, so she could spend just that little longer with her new love. However, Diogo was giving Marcelo a lift there, as he happened to be flying out to Argentina on business.

"I'll call you every day, I promise," Marcelo said.

"I'll be missing you terribly," Laura sniffled. "I'll be counting down the days 'til I see you again. I love you."

"I love you, too," Marcelo replied. "I miss you already!"

Laura blew Marcelo a loving kiss and drove back home with a sad smile curling her mouth. It was so very hard to say goodbye to Marcelo, but she knew they would soon be together again.

Chapter 7

Marcelo kept his promise to Laura and called her every day and every night; he wanted to be the first voice she heard in the morning upon waking, and the last one at night before she fell asleep with her heart happy and her head full of sweet dreams.

They had fallen madly and completely in love with one another—that much was certain. Both Laura and Marcelo counted the long days before they were to be together again.

It was a busy week for Laura. She spent most of her days in the Lisbon office with an overwhelming workload and the final preparations for attending the United Nations Gala Award Ceremony in New York. It had been a pleasant surprise for Laura to learn she was to receive an award for her prominent, vital role in promoting the most important values and objectives of the United Nations; her hard work and involvement in projects and initiatives to promote human rights had not gone unnoticed.

Laura, of course, had kept her sister informed about everything happening in her life, and had told her it would be the cherry on the cake to have Libby at the UN Award Gala dinner with her.

Sadly, however delighted Libby would have been to be there for Laura at such a special moment in her life, she had been forced to decline the invitation. Libby and Mark were just too busy with school commitments and exams, and it was not the right time for them to be taking time off. Libby told her sister she'd be thinking of her and made her promise to take plenty of pictures. She also asked when she would get to meet the wonderful Marcelo

"You will meet him soon, I promise," Laura told her. "I love you"

"I love you too, Laura".

The big day finally arrived. Laura packed her bags all ready to catch her flight to Marseille. A taxi picked her up at the door and drove her to Lisbon's Portela Airport. Her heart was in knots. The time hadn't flown as fast as she'd hoped it would. She had counted the seemly endless days, hours, and minutes to the day until she would see Marcelo again. It seemed like forever. The prospect of seeing Marcelo again made Laura so anxious and overwhelmed that she'd hardly slept the night before; she had missed him even more than she'd thought possible.

Laura was beyond excited to see Marcelo waiting for her at the airport with a beautiful bunch of flowers in his hand. She smiled broadly when she emerged through

the arrivals gate and espied her romantic, passionate French boyfriend, whose seductiveness charmed her completely.

"Laura!" he shouted across the concourse.

"Marcelo!" She ran toward him as quickly as her luggage would allow.

Finally together again, they kissed for the longest time. Holding hands with fingers entwined, they then headed out to the car park to where Marcelo's champagne-colored Bentley was parked. Ever the gentleman, he opened the car's door to help Laura in.

"Mmm, nice car." Laura took a good look around the inside of the luxurious car with its cream, soft leather seats and new car smell.

"I'm glad you like it," Marcelo said proudly. "It's basically new—I only bought it last month." Proud of his new baby, he smiled.

While Marcelo drove through Marseille, Laura took in the sights. "It's so very different from Paris—but also very beautiful," she said.

"It is. And when we have more time, I'll show you around. But, you have many more beautiful things to see..." Marcelo gently caressed Laura's hand with a twinkle in his eye.

"I'm sure of it," she replied with a sensual smile. "This really is a beautiful part of the country, Marcelo."

"I knew you'd like it," he said, "and there's so much more to see! You must be exhausted, though—I'll drive us straight home so you can unpack your bags and have a rest. Later on, I'll take you out to dinner and show you around a little."

"Yes, please!" Laura enthused. "That sounds perfect. I want to see *everything*."

"If we have the time," Marcelo said with a wink. "I have some business to take care of before we leave for New York."

"How is your business going?" Laura felt a little bad that she'd not asked him this sooner.

"Incredibly well," Marcelo replied. "We have business deals in progress with many foreign countries, and I just closed a huge contract with China."

"That's such a great market to be in," Laura said.

"Oh, yes, very much so," Marcelo said with a grin. "I'm very pleased with that particular deal! And what about you, Laura, are you all ready for the gala?"

"I am," Laura replied. "Especially since I just found out I'm to be presented with a Human Rights Prize award. It feels good to be recognized for doing the work I love. As a Human Rights Lawyer, protecting the most vulnerable and acting on their behalf is an honor for me; I'm glad to have made a difference for them" She tried her best to sound nonchalant, but her excitement shone through nonetheless.

"Wow, Laura! I am so proud of you!" Marcelo exclaimed. "This is so well deserved. We will have to celebrate!"

"It was a totally unexpected surprise." Laura beamed. "I'm just so happy you're coming with me to share the moment"

"I wouldn't miss it for the world. Besides which, you're my girl!" Marcelo sounded so happy. "Almost home!" he announced as he turned the car onto a narrow country road.

"It's actually getting prettier and prettier," Laura gasped as she peered through the window at the stunning Provence countryside.

The road leading to Marcelo's chateau boasted wonderfully charming views and proved to be quite breathtaking. From time to time, Laura would ask Marcelo to stop the car. She'd then climb out and take pictures of the picturesque views—especially of the dazzling lavender and sunflower fields, which had inspired Monet, Van Gogh, and many other impressionists across the years. "What an amazing source of inspiration," she said to Marcelo as she snapped away.

"I knew you'd love it!" He gave her his sweetest smile.

"How lucky am I for having such a handsome chauffeur to drive me around." Laura laughed. "And such a beautiful car to take me through this unbelievable scenery. I must say, this is a wonderfully informative guided tour by a charming Frenchman—what more could I ask for?"

Laura tenderly ran her fingers through her lover's hair as he drove on.

"So… I can assume I'm your complete package, Mademoiselle?" Marcelo joked.

"You are, my sweetheart, you are…"

Delighting in one another's company, Laura and Marcelo chatted and laughed together about the most trivial things, having agreed not talk about work anymore. "And what of your plans, Marcelo? What do you intend to do with me while I'm here?" Laura joked.

Marcel loved her sense of humor. "Oh my darling! You have no idea what I'm going to do with you." There was a cheeky twinkle in his eyes.

"Such as…?" she asked.

"Well, you know I love horse riding. I'm going to take you horse riding and show you the best of Provence. You'll love it"."

"I'm guessing you have horses?" Laura asked.

"Naturally."

"Are they friendly?" Laura sounded a tad nervous. "I have only ridden once—on a guided tour with a very calm and well-trained horse."

"You have nothing to worry about." Marcelo laughed. "My horses are very friendly. They normally do what I tell them, so as long as you behave, you'll be safe."

"Hmm… I'd better behave myself then." She laughed along.

At Laura's further request, they would pause their journey here and there for her to pop out of the car to take even more photographs of the spectacularly diverse landscapes that ran through the Verdon Gorge. "Whichever way I look, it's impossibly beautiful!" Laura declared in awe.

Marcelo took a little exit—finally they had reached their destination. He stopped for a moment in front of a magnificent wrought iron gate. "Here we are, my darling. We're home," he said as he turned to Laura.

They had arrived at Marcelo's family home—the superlative *Chateau Dubois*. A most imposing building, the chateau was a prime example of the classic architectural style from the late fifteen hundreds. Based on the French renaissance architecture, it featured elaborate towers, spiked spires, and steeply-pitched roofs; the whole place simply oozed a magical, fairytale charm, which left Laura holding her breath. *Chateau Dubois* was one of the oldest historic estates in the region. Surrounded by majestic pine trees and exquisite gardens, exuding elegance, refinement, and opulent wealth, it sat on twelve hundred and fifty acres of prime land between the sea and the Verdon River

Marcelo thumbed a button on the car's dashboard and the mighty gate swung open.

"I can't believe this is your home—it's *beautiful*," Laura said.

"*Oui, mon Cherie*, this is my *chateau*," said Marcelo with the biggest smile ever. He was clearly thrilled by Laura's rapt expression.

"Oh my Lord, this is *really* impressive… it's quite surreal, Marcelo!" Laura's eyes were wide open and her jaw dropped. "This has to be the most beautiful house in the world."

The Frenchman nodded. "It has been in my family for many generations—ever since the sixteenth century."

An impeccably dressed butler—a distinguished-looking man in his late sixties—waited for them in front of the solid oak front door.

"Good afternoon, sir," he said as Marcelo and Laura got out of the Bentley.

"Laura, this is Pierre." Marcelo made the introduction. "Pierre has been with our family since before I was born."

"Hello, it's nice to meet you, Pierre." Laura held out her hand for the butler to shake.

"Mademoiselle," Pierre responded politely. "How do you do?"

As Pierre ushered Laura and Marcelo into the chateau, Marcelo told Laura that the old butler was like family to him. Pierre only treated him with such formality when there were guests, or in the presence of the other chateau staff. When they were alone, Pierre always called him Marcelo, which was just as the young man preferred it.

"That's so lovely of you," Laura said.

"He was very reluctant at the beginning," Marcelo explained. "Pierre is very old school when it comes to etiquette. He got used to the idea eventually, though." He grasped Laura's hand. "Come, it's my turn to show you around *my* home."

A delighted Laura looked around the exquisite, eleven-bedroom chateau with its abundance of antique furniture and wood-beamed, high ceilings; the whole place was wonderfully furnished with every conceivable stylish modern comfort. In the center of the back wall of the immense dining area, an antique mirror sat high above the gorgeous fireplace. It was there Laura noticed the painting she'd given to Marcelo—it took pride of place next to the natural stone fireplace. Marcelo had framed her painting with a vintage gilt frame, which was speckled with telltale signs of age. It added wonderfully to the warm sense of history in the lavish room. Laura paused to admire the painting. "It's perfectly framed," she said. "The wood certainly brings out the best in the picture."

"The picture brings out the best in me every time I look at it," Marcelo replied.

"Our lake..."

"Where the magic happened." Marcelo completed her sentence with a loving smile. "Come, I'll show you our bedroom—you can see the rest of the house tomorrow."

"That's a good idea," Laura agreed. "I wouldn't attempt to see all of your house in one day!"

"Don't worry, you'll get used to it."

Upon arriving at the bedroom, Laura looked deep into Marcelo's eyes and said, "So… you are a prince, and this is your castle."

Marcelo nodded. "But my castle is empty without you, my princess," he said tenderly. Then, embracing tightly, they shared a passionate kiss and made their way to the expansive bed to abandon their bodies to one another.

Before leaving for New York, Marcelo and Laura spent their time relaxing in the chateau's many delightful outdoor areas. They enjoyed swimming together in the large, crystal blue pool, toasting the summer sunsets, and walking hand-in-hand through the countless acres of vineyards. And as time went along, they grew closer and closer as their romance blossomed even more.

There was a stable behind the vineyard, which was home to Marcelo's white Camargue horses. One of the things Laura and Marcelo enjoyed the most was to go horse riding deep into the forests and limestone hills around the chateau to see the herds of the iconic wild horses that were native to the area.

"I'm besotted by it all," Laura declared. "I can't find a better word—this is totally amazing!"

Marcelo also showed Laura the very best of his country. Holding hands, they strolled the many streets of the beautiful small towns that peppered Provence. And, together, they relished the caress of the gentle breeze against their faces as, around each corner, they were greeted by yet more picturesque scenery.

On their last night before leaving for New York, Marcelo organized an intimate dinner for two at the chateau. Leaving no detail overlooked, the table was set with the most exquisite tableware and positioned beneath the baroque chandelier, which added an elegantly romantic sparkle to the room. There were red roses, antique, gold-rimmed plates, solid silver cutlery, and shining crystal glasses. The glow from the fat, flickering candles on their antique silver sticks shimmered out of the French windows into the night, and was accompanied by the gentle strains of classical music—the ambiance was nothing less than magical.

Served by immaculately dressed, exceedingly polite waiters, Marcelo and Laura savored an exquisite French dinner prepared by Marcelo's chef, Louis, which was accompanied by a selection of very special wines—all selected from the chateau's extensive wine cellar by Marcelo himself.

"This is simply delightful," Laura purred. "Thank you so much, my love."

"It was totally my pleasure, darling," Marcelo replied as he gazed lovingly into Laura's eyes.

After dinner, they moved to a cozy, more intimate sitting room. Seated comfortably on the stylish French sofa, Laura enjoyed a freshly prepared martini as Marcelo sipped at a single malt whiskey on the rocks. Holding Laura's hands in his, Marcelo declared, "I truly love you, Laura. I want you to be part of my life forever. I don't want us ever to be apart again; I want you here, my love, forever with me."

Then Marcelo slid from the sofa and bent down on one knee in front of Laura. He opened a small, velvet-covered box he'd had secreted in his pocket. It contained the most beautiful yellow diamond ring Laura had ever seen.

"Will you be my wife?" he asked.

Taken totally by surprise, Laura, looking stunning in an adorable white lace dress, placed a hand over her heart and looked deep into Marcelo's eyes. A single tear of joy rolled down her face as she gave her answer, "Yes, Marcelo, yes! I love you, Marcelo! I adore you, my love!"

"I'm so happy I found you, Laura. I was lost without you!"

"And I was lost without you, my love!"

And with that, they kissed...

Chapter 8

They departed for New York mid-morning. Marcelo had made all the arrangements for the flight, and, since they were going straight from the airport to the United Nations Gala Awards, they would be both changing into their appropriate gala attire in the jet just before landing.

For the nine-and-a-half-hour flight, Laura opted for a comfortable but oh so stylish three-quarter sleeve, laced mini dress in mustard. She accessorized it with brown suede boho sandals and a matching brown leather bag, which she flung casually over her shoulder. Marcelo looked effortlessly stylish in his traditional French beret, black square-framed sunglasses, a navy polo, washed out jeans, and taupe swede shoes.

At the front of Marcelo's chateau, a white limousine awaited them. Marcelo's staff looked on fondly as he and Laura departed—they were all absolutely delighted by the sight of Laura on their boss's arm, and thrilled to bear witness to the happiness of the young man they'd known since he was a young boy. He'd invited many girlfriends to the chateau before—most just the once—but they'd known Laura was different from the very first time they'd laid eyes on her.

After a little while, they arrived at the airport. The chauffeur pulled the limousine up near a Gulf Steam G650ER private jet that sat on a secluded corner of the airport. He got out and opened the car's door for Laura. She climbed out and looked every inch the Hollywood superstar as she walked arm in arm with Marcelo across the red carpet that had been laid out for them.

At the top of the jet's stairs, the captain welcomed them with a smile and a salute.

Making herself comfortable, Laura took the time to take a good look around the luxury jet. It had modern design concepts and looked sleek and minimalist in its white color scheme. Lost for words, her eyes shining, Laura looked at Marcelo and gave him a beautiful smile.

As planned, before landing in New York, where another white limousine was standing by to take Laura and Marcelo to the Gala Award Ceremony, they changed into their glamorous outfits.

Laura wore a beautifully long, silky, deep-navy gown with a low V-neck, three-quarter sleeves, and exotically delicate lace appliqués. To further embody her elegance, Laura wore the luxurious jewelry Marcelo had given her from his family's collection. This comprised a stunning sixteenth-century necklace with blue diamonds surrounded by small, white diamonds, along with matching pendant earrings—simply the perfect accompaniment for Laura's exquisite dress.

Laura had barely believed her eyes when Marcelo opened the navy blue, velvet box to present her with the exquisite set. "They have been in my family for generations. They've been passed down from mother to daughter—these belonged to my late mother, and I wanted you to have them," he'd said as he placed the beautiful necklace around her neck.

Putting on the earrings, Laura looked at herself in the mirror. "This is such an honor." She turned to Marcelo with love in her eyes. "Thank you so much. You're going to make me cry. This must mean a lot to you."

"It does—and so do you. You are all I ever wanted," Marcelo replied with a smile. "They suit you perfectly."

When they arrived at the gala venue, it was already packed with myriad distinguished guests in all their splendor. The chauffeur opened Laura's door and, arm in arm with Marcelo, she walked across the red carpet. In her gorgeously elegant dress and stunning jewelry, Laura absolutely shone—especially on the arm of her handsome Prince Charming in his tuxedo. It was indeed a pure Cinderella moment!

The evening was just perfect for Laura. She was surrounded by the rich and famous, the influential, and the beautiful—all talking and laughing while the paparazzi buzzed amongst them to snap pictures of the innumerable world-renowned personalities. Laura found it ironic to think that if that heartbreak hadn't happened, she would never have met Marcelo and discovered a love so unique, so beautiful, a love so sublime that withstands the test of time. Any doubts and trust issues she harbored in her soul had gone the moment Marcelo swept her off her feet. Theirs was, indeed, a union made by the magic of the lake in Sintra.

On Marcelo's arm, exuding pure confidence, Laura walked into the gala. Smiling to herself, Laura gazed lovingly at the man she had fallen so helplessly in love with. She thought he looked every inch the perfect gentleman. The lovely gypsy woman she'd met on the street corner in Sintra during the music festival sprang into her mind. She'd been right all along—Laura *had* found her prince!

The elegantly decorated Grand Ballroom, with its huge windows offering breathtaking views across the city, was the perfect setting for the lavish dinner menu of crab entrée, French style stuffed chicken breast, and a delicious mango tarte brushed in honey.

Dinner was followed by the awards ceremony itself, and before too long, it was Laura's turn to receive hers. It sounded so incredibly surreal to hear her name as it was read out and the Master of Ceremonies invited *Laura Menzies* up to the podium. As Laura stood up, Marcelo smiled his encouragement and gave her fingers a little squeeze.

"Please accept this award as a token of the United Nation's appreciation for your consistent and outstanding contribution for the promotion of the Human Rights. You are a dedicated and valued member of this organization who has stood at the front line of human suffering, helped combat global poverty, and raised awareness of terrible human tragedies. It is people such as you that make us great. Thank you, Laura Menzies".

Well prepared as always, Laura delivered a brief yet moving speech, which received a standing ovation and enthusiastic applause. She accepted with grace the "Prize of the Human Rights Field" and expressed her infinite gratitude. "Thank you for the privilege and opportunity given to me by the United Nations. I praise the organization I proudly represent for its amazing projects, many of which I have had the privilege to be a part of. I am humbled to be the recipient of this award on behalf of myself and my loyal, dedicated, and most valued team. Thank you."

Like Laura, everyone in that room of talented individuals had played a vital role within the UN to help the global community advance peace, prosperity, and justice.

Overwhelmed, Marcelo's broad chest puffed out with pride beneath his tuxedo as he enthusiastically applauded the girl he'd first met in the impossibly beautiful Valley of Lakes in Sintra. The dazzling woman up there on the podium had conquered his heart and was soon to be his wife.

Laura left the stage with the applause ringing in her ears. Marcelo took her hand and held it tight. "I've got you," he whispered in her ear.

Just like in a fairytale he once knew by heart, since the very first time he'd laid eyes on Laura he'd known he'd found *The One*. As for Laura, she felt like the planets and the universe had finally aligned for her; when she looked into Marcelo's eyes, she just knew she was home and finally felt whole, complete.

With all that had happened in her life, Laura would never have guessed she would discover a love so unique, so beautiful, and like no other she'd ever experienced before. Any doubts and trust issues that lurked in Laura's soul had vanished the moment Marcelo swept her off her feet; he brought out the very best in her, and she brought out the best in him. Theirs was, indeed, a union woven by the magic of that beautiful lake in Sintra. It had cast its spell on them—one of *Happily Ever After*.

The End

Author Brief

Delia Dibble was born in Madeira Island, Portugal in 1958. She grew up in Angola and due to the civil war she returned to Portugal in 1974. She worked at the Presidency of Madeira Island and studied History at Classic University in Lisbon. She came to Australia in 1987 on a diplomatic visa and held the position of Head of Social and Cultural Services at the Consulate General of Portugal in Sydney.

She is an avid traveller where she likes to journal the rich tapestry that our beautiful world has to offer. It is her professional and personal experience that allows her to add colour to her work. *Secrets on the Lake* is her first published novel.

She lives on a beautiful island east of Australia.